10 Holiday Stories

A Collection

Dara Girard

ILORI
Press Books, LLC

Table of Contents

The Special Guest

"She's daft, she is," Mary Marshall said as she set the dining room table for four.

"Mum, keep your voice down," her daughter Eva replied as she placed an elegantly designed napkin on the table.

"Why? She can't hear me, with her banging on in the kitchen like that. Acting as if she were expecting the bleeding queen," Mary said with a careless shrug, her words thick with a northern English accent she hadn't been able to drop after living nearly thirty years in the United States. Although, not much else about her had changed from the twenty-two year old new bride who'd settled with her husband in Hamsford, Maryland. Her figure had thickened after three children and only her hairdresser knew she was now completely grey. She dyed her shoulder-length hair a light brown to complement her soft cocoa colored skin.

"Mum, shh," Eva said with warning. She only called her mother 'mum' when she was annoyed with her. At twenty-five, she was slender and lovely, with skin that matched her mother's, and flashing brown eyes.

"You know we're no better egging her on this way."

"We're her friends."

"Aren't friends 'pose to tell each other the truth? We know that no good nephew of hers won't show up no matter how much she wants him to. Your father had the sense to stay away, and we're likely as daft as she is."

"John said he would come," Eva said, straightening a fork.

Her mother sniffed. "And you believe that?"

It was more likely that Father Christmas would come to visit than John, but Eva didn't want to admit it for her friend's sake. "It's not what we believe, it's what she does."

"Maybe the no good bastard might do us a favor and do the decent thing. That'd be a miracle, wouldn't it? Poor woman could use one."

Fortunately, Miranda Simmonds, the topic of their conversation, couldn't hear what the two women were saying. Her heart was too full of joy. Her dear nephew, John Washer, said he'd come and spend time with her over the holidays. He was the only family she had left who bothered to take any notice of her. Her sister had married for a fourth time, and lived in Trinidad, her nieces had little use for her, but John was different. For five years she'd cared for him, while her older sister got her life together after a cancer diagnosis and an addiction to pain pills.

Miranda had provided John with a stable home that his parents hadn't been able to provide. With the help of her father, she'd helped care for John from the ages of six to eleven. She'd worked with her father at the hardware store he'd started. More often than not, she'd had to get between grandfather and grandson because they were both strong-willed men, but she hadn't minded. Family was important to her.

But after her sister improved, and John went back to live with her, they'd lost touch. He'd been a rambunctious boy, but she'd found him more inquisitive than annoying. No one had expected much from him, but he'd surprised them. He was a soldier and achieved the rank of staff sergeant. She felt that his desire to serve may have had a little to do with the years she'd raised him. She'd instilled in him the importance of a life of giving to others. She'd taken him with her to volunteer at the local homeless shelter, to deliver a turkey every Thanksgiving, or donate clothing or toys he no longer needed. She'd not wanted him to be like his parents, who'd barely looked past themselves to even recognize that they had a son, and later, two daughters.

And now he was coming to see her after so many years. It wouldn't be another empty holiday. She'd had a series of them since her father's passing three years ago. Her sister was always too busy to schedule a time to visit, but that didn't matter now.

This year she wouldn't be a charity guest, although she knew her friends meant well. She wanted to return the favor and host a family dinner for them, and now she could. John was one of the lucky ones to come home from the war unscathed, though she didn't know how his mind might be. She wouldn't ask too many questions. She was just glad she had family to share the holiday with again.

It was kind of her neighbors to agree to come. It was a week before Christmas and she'd wanted to make it special. In several days they'd be leaving for New York to be with their family.

Miranda cast an anxious glance at the clock. He'd be there any minute, she thought, as she cast a look over the food.

Spices scented the bright, airy kitchen, which hosted toasted hardo bread, limeade, mashed potatoes, sweet potatoes, a turkey that was browning in the oven, fried plantain and an assortment of cookies and a cake. She could imagine the look of delight on John's face as he piled his plate high with food. "Oh, pumpkin pie, my favorite. I can't believe you remembered," he'd say. And she'd grin and not let him know that she hadn't forgotten anything he enjoyed.

Her phone alerted her to a text, waking her from her daydream. She glanced down and her heart stopped.

Won't be able to make it. Sorry, Auntie.

Miranda read the text four times. No…five, then six times. It had to be a mistake. Or maybe a joke. As a boy, John was known for his silly jokes. He'd knock on the front door any minute and laugh. And she'd playfully hit him in the shoulder and scold him for scaring her. She waited.

But the knock at the door didn't come.

Why couldn't he make it? Why would he cancel a few minutes before he was supposed to arrive? The message had to be wrong. She texted him back.

If you're running late, I can keep the food warm.

Sorry, Auntie. Another time.

Sorry, Auntie. She could almost hear the casual, dismissive way he'd say it. He'd said it so many times before. 'Sorry Auntie, I couldn't help myself,' he'd say when she found he'd eaten a pie she'd meant for a guest, 'Sorry Auntie,' he'd say when he'd broken a new vase she'd brought, or when she'd told him not to play with his ball in the house, or when he'd leave jelly stains all over her father's woodworking magazine. Sorry, sorry, sorry. Always sorry.

But she was sorrier still. Sorry that she'd told her neighbors he was coming, even boasting to her employees at work. She usually didn't have any news. She'd devoted most of her life to her father—a man who'd been her best friend—and their store. That dedication hadn't bothered her until his passing, leaving an emptiness in her life. But her nephew's upcoming visit had given her something interesting to share—and some attention—at least for a little while.

Attention usually passed her by. She knew many residents of Hamsford felt sorry for her. She was an example of what *not* to do with one's life. A cautionary tale for young women. "If you don't find a man now, you'll end up a spinster like Miranda." "Don't work so hard or you'll end up like Miranda." "Be careful not to give so much or you'll end up an old maid like Miranda."

She couldn't blame them and usually didn't mind the chatter. Nobody had expected much from her, even when she was young. She'd never been a beauty—more handsome than pretty, with chestnut brown skin and dark brown eyes. And now, pushing forty, she knew her options were limited, but she didn't regret her life. Except when the holidays came, shining a light on her loneliness, but not this time. This holiday was going to be different because her nephew—a *soldier*—was coming home for the holidays. And her colleagues had been pleased for her, they'd even given her a card and money to give to him. Thanking him for his service.

What would she tell them now?

Mary came into the kitchen. "It's getting late. Take off your apron and fix your hair," she said, glancing at the untidy bun at the top of Miranda's head.

"I forgot something," Miranda said, feeling the need to escape. To think. To plan. She couldn't tell them yet. She didn't want them to feel sorry for her. Not again. "I have to go to the store and—"

"But there's no time."

Miranda hung up her apron. "I'll only be a minute."

"I'll go. Eva brought that scarf you wanted to borrow and—"

"No, no, you stay here," Miranda said turning away, tears building. Their kindness hurt her. They were so good to her. Couldn't John have come at least for them? He and

Eva had played together when they were younger. Couldn't he have made an appearance for her? She'd even entertained a vague hope that they'd get on since they were both still single.

Miranda left the kitchen and raced past Eva. She grabbed her coat. "Won't be a minute," she said again before grabbing her car keys and leaving.

Chapter Two

She drove, not knowing where, or for how long. She didn't have much time. She couldn't leave Mary and Eva waiting forever. But how could she face them? "I told you so," Mary would say. "Didn't I say that nephew of yours was no good?" Eva would just look at her with pity. It was all so humiliating! But she knew she had to go back; running away wouldn't solve anything. *Oh Dad, I wish you could help me. I miss you so much,* she thought, holding back tears. She had no other choice. She'd wrap up all the food and send Mary and Eva home. She'd lost her appetite anyway.

Miranda slowed her car and stopped at the empty four-way intersection then quickly turned to head back home just as a young man in uniform stepped off the curb into the crosswalk. She braked quickly, but not soon enough. She felt the thud, saw him fall and her heart dropped.

She jumped out of the car and raced over to him, grateful not to see any blood.

The man sat up, looking dazed.

"I'm so sorry," she said, kneeling beside him.

"Serves me right," he said, standing. "I wasn't looking where I was going."

That was true, but that didn't make her feel any better. She stood too, but he was nearly a foot taller than she was so she had to look up at him. He was young, though there was a cool cynicism to his features that belonged on a man much older. "Do you need to go to a hospital?" she asked.

"No, I'm fine really." He dusted off his pants, although the action did nothing to make them look less worn. "What? You've never seen a man fall on his pride before?"

Miranda looked him over to make sure he was really okay. He had skin the color of rye bread and his face didn't appear kind. Perhaps, if he'd had more pleasant features she would have left him alone, but his biting brown eyes and sharp arrogant jaw made her think of her father when he was in one of his gruff moods or when a customer was ready to voice a complaint. She'd spent years soothing over such moments. A handsome, pleasant stranger would have made her flustered, but this irritated stranger with his sarcastic tone made her feel more relaxed.

"At least let me take you where you were going," she said. "I can drop you there."

He looked over her head at something in the distance, making it clear he wanted to be somewhere else. "I'm not going anywhere really."

"Where are you staying?"

He shrugged. "Haven't figured that out yet either."

Miranda folded her arms. "You're not from around here."

He met her gaze and for a moment a glint of humor lit his dark gaze, shedding the anger and cynicism and the years, making him appear younger than he had looked before. "What gave me away?"

The uniform for one. It was ill-fitted. Most of the Hamsford men who'd chosen to fight wore their uniform with an arrogance, as if to compensate for a sense of divided loyalties. Hamsford was a community filled with immigrants, some not sure if their sacrifice meant much to their new home country. There were still those in their adopted homeland who saw them as outsiders no matter how much blood they shed on battlefields abroad.

But this young man looked dejected. Defeated. Haunted. "Are you sure you're all right?"

"I'm fine, really," he said, then his stomach grumbled.

Miranda couldn't help a smile. "You're hungry."

He folded his arms, his frown increasing. "Well, I'm fine aside from that."

She bit her lip, looking him up and down. He was just the right age, height and look. And if she did him a favor…

"I've got a hot meal waiting," she said, "if you'd just do one thing for me."

"What?" he asked with caution.

"Pretend to be my nephew just for one evening."

His hands fell to his side. "But I'm—"

She clasped her hands together. "Please, just for an hour maybe two. All you'd have to do is stuff your mouth with oven roasted turkey, browned to a crisp succulent sheen, but if you're vegetarian," she quickly added when he started to speak, "I also have mashed potatoes with chives, a bean salad medley, fried plantain and—"

His stomach growled louder.

She grinned. "Is that a yes?"

He frowned. "You're a cruel woman."

"No, just a desperate one. This isn't a time for pride. I owe you anyway. I nearly ran you down."

"No, I walked into the street without looking."

"Yes, exactly," she said snapping her fingers. She ran her hand over an invisible dent on the hood. "See that damage? That's your fault. What are you going to do about it?"

A slight smile touched the corner of his hard mouth. "Fine, I'll be your nephew."

Miranda opened the passenger side door. "Good, thank you. Your name is John."

He sat inside and pulled on his seatbelt with a groan. "Please don't tell me you call me Johnny."

"No, but Ms. Mary sometimes calls you Jay."

He froze. "How many other people will be there?"

"Just two," Miranda said starting the car. She glanced at the clock. She'd met this stranger just in time.

He tapped a beat on his knee. "I'm not much of an actor."

"You don't have to remember much. I'll cover for you. It was so long ago that you were here I doubt they'll expect much from you. Just keep your mouth full and nod and you should be fine. And you can talk about your time abroad if you want, but there's no pressure."

"And what do I call you?"

"Just call me Auntie."

Chapter Three

Brett Greenwood stared at his reflection in the pristine bathroom mirror, wondering how he'd gotten into this mess.

He looked terrible. His uniform was worn and big. Why would she want to present someone like him? But he was hungry and if this was the price of a good meal, he'd do it with a smile, even though he hadn't felt like smiling for a long time. At twenty-eight, he felt decades older. Only a couple of hours ago he'd been on a bus leaving New Jersey heading south, not caring where he ended up. Twice, strangers had thanked him for his service and sacrifice. One little boy called him a hero. But he knew he wasn't.

He barely felt like a man. He didn't want to feel at all. After losing his savings in a business deal that had gone bad, he'd paid back his best friend, Leonard, who'd loaned him some money, only to discover he'd lost more than that.

He'd gone to Leonard's office to repay him and was told he was out of the office. And he'd believed the receptionist before he caught Leonard coming out of a utility closet with Sarah—Brett's girlfriend—both of them adjusting their attire. If it had been someone else, he would have found it funny. Sarah didn't even use the ladies' room and never took public transport, and yet this was where they'd decided to be intimate.

He just stared at them, hardly hearing their excuses as they tumbled out of their mouths like rice spilling out the bottom of a bag.

"We were going to tell you."

"It's not what you think."

"It hurt us too."

"Look, we didn't mean it to happen."

He couldn't even remember who said what; he was just afraid he was going to be sick. Since grade school, Leonard had been like a brother to him. He looked chagrined, but nothing more. Sarah had tears shining in her eyes, her dusty skin red from embarrassment, guilt or exertion. Considering what they'd been up to, he wasn't sure.

What hurt most was that she'd made it clear he hadn't been worth waiting for. She couldn't even wait two years for him. The woman he'd planned to marry, to spend his life with, had traded him in for his best friend and his six-figure salary.

"We got involved around the time when…when we feared you were dead," Sarah said. "I turned to him for comfort."

"And after you found out I was okay?" Brett managed to say, his tongue feeling like a lead weight in his mouth.

"It was too late," Leonard said.

"We couldn't tell you," Sarah added.

He felt like such a fool. All those online talks, texts, emails. They'd been lies. He'd stayed true, when lots of his other pals hadn't, and this had been his reward.

After paying Leonard what he owed, Brett had two hundred dollars left and decided to catch a bus.

"Where are you heading?" an older man with an island accent asked him in the bus depot while they both stood in line.

The man's voice was soft, like a whisper, but Brett could hear it despite the sound of a baby crying, wheels of luggage carts dragging along the ground, and discordant conversations. "Doesn't matter, I just want to be away."

"Then you should go to Hamsford."

Brett met the man's eyes, a little surprised by their intensity. He was a large, dark-skinned man with a trim white beard. "Is that where you're going?"

"No, but you just look like a man who needs some peace."

How right he was, Brett thought, but he still hesitated.

The man nudged him with his elbow. "Go nuh. What you haffi lose?"

Brett took a deep breath, then impulsively bought a ticket. He left without any luggage or even an overcoat. He just needed to get out of the city, to get away from the memories, from his failed plans.

Hours later he got off in Hamsford, a place he'd only known vaguely about because of a store his father used to talk about here. Brett walked around in the cool air, listening to the different accents, many reminding him of the stranger and his own Jamaican parents who'd left him too soon. He briefly thought about his father, who was a foot shorter than him, and who'd liked to pat him on the back and affectionately say, "How's my little boy?" It was a silly joke that had always made him smile; his mother would just shake her head. She was as small as his father. Whenever they stood on either side of him, they looked like the perfect bookends. And before their passing, he'd wanted to scoop them up and carry them around with him. With them he'd never felt alone, he'd always felt loved. Now he had no one to keep his loneliness at bay.

He missed them. He missed them so much it ached. He felt the sting of tears. He'd hope to come home to Sarah, but now knew he'd spend the holidays alone.

Alone with the bitter crumbs of dashed hopes. He walked around the streets of Hamsford as a cool evening sun painted the sky in pastel hues. He passed a food market, the scent of vegetable patties and cumin wafting towards him, reminding him that he'd left without eating anything. He shuffled by a row of small stores, children riding their bicycles, and a man chasing after a rooster that had no business being there. He made his way onto a residential street, the sights of the neatly lined homes twisting a knife into his heart. He'd hoped to have a home like this with Sarah. He decided to keep his head down and block out the sights around him. He didn't want to see the well-manicured lawns, or the holiday decorations. That's when he'd stepped into the road.

After being struck, his first instinct was to be angry. He wanted to be mad, he wanted to get into a fight and had a man gotten out of the car, he probably would have. He'd felt like smashing his fist into someone's face. A violent, primitive rage seized him, but it quickly disappeared when he saw her.

A woman who stared down at him as if she'd run over a family of ducklings. For a moment that annoyed him because she cared and he didn't want her to. He wanted her to go away and leave him alone. Instead, he found himself drawn in by her warm brown eyes. People didn't usually look at him like that. They usually saw a threat, but not her. No matter how cutting or surly he seemed, she wouldn't leave, forcing him—to his annoyance—to notice how pretty she was. And then she'd asked for a crazy favor and he'd said yes.

With a shake of his head, Brett wiped his dirty face and large, cold hands with the fragrant scented soap and warm water.

Minutes later he sat at the head of a table, which seemed to groan under the weight of many dishes, while three women stared at the man he was supposed to be—Staff Sergeant John Washer. He'd run away from one woman and ended up in the presence of three. Fate had a funny sense of humor.

Chapter Four

She wouldn't have recognized him, Eva thought as she stared at John. He didn't look anything like the boy she'd used to run from. And where had his vanity gone? Her mother used to call him Mr. O'Jay referring to a polished singing group the O'Jays from the past. 'Look it up,' she liked to tell him. John would never have worn a uniform that didn't fit him before. But perhaps the years overseas had changed him. That was possible. Although she doubted it. There was something she didn't trust about him.

"Remember when we used to play that video game and every time you scored you'd punch me in the arm?" she asked him.

"What's past is past," Miranda said.

"I remember it clearly," Eva said, helping herself to another roll. "Just wondered if he did."

"I guess I wasn't the nicest kid," he said without apology.

Eva frowned. Even his voice didn't seem to match what she remembered. Although she didn't know how John sounded now, she'd never imagined his dark, sarcastic edge. John was always about charm. That's why he got into trouble with little consequence. However, this large, grim man looked as if he'd spent half his life facing the corner. "Think you're better now, soldier?"

"I hope so."

"We weren't even sure you'd make an appearance," Mary said, giving Eva a stern look. "So that's an improvement."

Eva stared at her mother, surprised. She usually was more suspicious of people than Eva was, but she'd smiled with pleasure when John gruffly complimented her spicy rice. However, Eva wouldn't be as easily swayed no matter how handsome he was. She sensed something off—something wrong. Ms. Miranda was too dear to her for her to ignore her instincts. She hoped John wouldn't stay long. That he'd spend one night in the little guest room Ms. Miranda so lovingly put together—newly painted, aired, scented with a fresh bouquet of flowers—and then disappear out of her life.

Chapter Five

"You're doing great," Miranda said when Brett offered to help her in the kitchen 'Like you used to,' she'd added so that Eva and Mary wouldn't offer. Although they all knew that John rarely helped her and only did so reluctantly.

"Eva doesn't like me," he said.

"No," Miranda agreed with a laugh. "So you must be doing something right, she didn't get on well with John either. Unless…"

Brett raised a brow at the sudden worried look on her face. "Unless what?"

"Unless you wanted her to like you. I'm sorry, I never saw this from your point of view. Eva is a very attractive young woman and she's single. I had thought maybe she and John, but with you here maybe—"

Brett shook his head. "Nope, I'm not interested. I'm off women for now."

"You're too young to be off women."

"I'm not interested." He took a bowl and placed it on a high shelf.

Miranda pointed at it. "That doesn't go there."

"I know. Promise you won't try to set me up with Eva."

"Why would I—"

"Promise."

A sly grin touched her mouth. "I could just get a stool."

"I'm warning you, *Auntie.*"

She laughed. "I know. Stop looking so fierce."

Brett blinked surprised. Usually his tough expression put people on edge, but Miranda looked amused. He couldn't understand why he didn't frighten her, but her response helped his tension ebb. She felt comfortable with him and he was starting to feel the same with her. "Did John ever have an uncle?" he asked, briefly wondering why there was no sign of a man around.

"What?"

"Nothing," he said feeling stupid. Just because there was no man in the house, didn't mean she was single. She could be dating. He silently swore. He had no business thinking about whether she was in a relationship or not. He wasn't interested in Eva and he wasn't interest in her. "You haven't promised me yet."

Her eyes twinkled. "I promise."

He frowned, feeling his heart pick up pace and not knowing why. "How come I don't trust you?"

Her smile widened. "I don't know."

He didn't believe her, but Miranda got him wondering about something he didn't want to. Eva was attractive, smart, and clearly cared about her friend. But she rubbed him wrong. Reminded him too much of Sarah. Plus, he didn't like how she looked at him, no—studied him— assessed him. He didn't want to ruin Miranda's evening and hated Eva's questions trying to trip him up. He wouldn't fail for Miranda's sake, although he wanted to give Eva a piece of his mind. He also wished he had a chance to meet the nephew who didn't deserve the aunt he had.

"What do you find so amusing?" he asked instead.

"You're cute when you're shy."

He took another bowl and put it on the high shelf to annoy her, feeling his face burn. "I'm not shy."

"Okay. I promise I won't say a word."

And to his relief, Miranda kept her promise and let him endure Eva's biting tongue and wary glances without trying to match them up. Then the evening was over and the two women were gone, leaving him alone with Miranda in her living room with coffee and cake. They sat in front of an unlit fire, the lights from her Christmas tree and garlands lit with an assortment of colors.

"What brought you to Hamsford?" she asked.

He didn't want to tell her about something that was still too painful to admit. "My father liked to order stuff from a hardware store around here."

Miranda sat up. "Simmonds Hardware?"

"Yes, that's it."

"That's my store," she said, tapping her chest in excitement. "It was started by my father. He always loved fixing things. Your father was a client?"

"For years," Brett said, then told her his name.

"That's wonderful! I'll have to look him up in my father's notes. Your father liked building things too?"

"Yes," Brett said with a groan. "Badly."

She laughed. "How is he?"

He sighed. "Gone."

She refilled his cup. "Mine too." She stood. "Wait here." She left the room, then came back with an oversized, green journal. "These are my father's notes," she said, taking a seat beside Brett so she could show him. "He liked to write down things about clients so that he would remember them because each one was important to him. I think I remember him mentioning your father's name." She flipped through the journal's yellowed pages then stopped. "Your father was a tool addict."

Brett couldn't help a laugh. "Yes, anything new and he'd buy it."

"Good man," Miranda said, reading her father's notes. "Loves his wife and son, a boy named Brett. Remember birthday."

Brett nodded. "Yep, it's your father's fault that I'd get a gift card every year to buy something that my father would use to make a horrible mess."

"I'm sorry."

"Don't be, it made him happy and I learned early on how to make repairs. If you have anything broken," he tapped his chest, "I'm your man."

"I'll remember that," Miranda said, suddenly wanting to remember everything about him. She soon became aware of how close they were, felt the heat of his leg as it touched hers. Before she hadn't noticed the size of his hands, the breadth of his shoulders, the dark brown of his eyes that reminded her of rum cake.

Miranda hastily shifted her gaze and looked at the clock. "It's late. Do you have somewhere to stay tonight?"

"No," Brett said, looking at another note her father had written. "Just drop me back at the bus depot."

Miranda licked her lips, wishing she wasn't so aware of how his body pressed against her side as he bent to look at the journal. "I don't think the buses are still running."

He shrugged, his gaze still focused on the journal. "That's fine. I'll stay there until morning and then I'll—"

She briefly closed her eyes, gathering her courage. "I have a room already made for John, but you can use it instead."

Brett's head shot up. "You don't even know me."

Miranda tapped the journal. "My father did. You're practically family," she continued when he hesitated. "And I owe you for hitting you with my car." He stared at her for a long moment, until Miranda grew uncomfortable. Did he think she was crazy? Maybe she was, but for some reason she didn't want to say goodbye yet. "What?"

"You're too trusting." He held out his hand. "Give me your cell phone."

Miranda handed him her phone, confused. "Why?"

"I'm giving you my full name, phone number and address," he said, putting the information in her address book. "If anything happened to you, they'd know the last person you were with."

"Nothing's going to happen to me," Miranda said, surprised by his serious tone.

"You don't know with strangers." He handed the cell phone back to her. "I am trustworthy, but not everyone is, so promise me you won't make an offer like this to someone else."

Miranda folded her arms amused. "You're really big into promises, aren't you?"

"Especially when they're kept."

She affectionately patted him on the shoulder. "You can relax. You're the first and last strange man I've asked to stay in my guest room."

"Good."

"Does that mean you're staying?"

He sighed. "I shouldn't."

Miranda grinned. "I'll take that as a yes."

Chapter Six

What am I doing? Brett wondered as he paced the small guest room. Why did he keep saying yes to her? This wasn't like him. He should be waiting at the bus depot or staying in some motel somewhere, not in a cozy little room with freshly laundered sheets.

He heard a light tap on the door. "Is everything okay?"

"I'm fine," he said, glancing down at the pajamas she'd given him to wear. It was a pair of her father's that fit surprisingly well. He'd never been able to borrow anything from his father.

"Let me know if you need anything."

"I just need to sleep," he said, climbing into bed, hoping he'd be able to.

***

He slept better than expected and woke up the next morning so rejuvenated that he offered to chop vegetables for the omelet Miranda planned to make for breakfast. For some reason he felt a slight anticipation of something, but he didn't know what. He focused on his task, thinking of what ingredients Miranda would add, then his mind drifted to Sarah. She'd been a master in the kitchen, chopping fast and efficiently. She'd once made him a dish he couldn't pronounce. Some French dish. Or was it Spanish? She spoke both languages fluently. He'd learned Portuguese from his maternal grandfather. Sarah used to tease him about why he had such a dull English name when he had such a rich ethnic heritage. He'd never told her his mother had named him after a hero she'd read in a novel.

Hero. Sarah would laugh at the word. He wasn't her hero and there'd be no happily ever after ending. He'd stopped believing in those.

He was so lost in thought that when he sliced through his finger, right down to the bone, he didn't feel the pain at first. He just saw the blood and felt anger at his own stupidity. Some soldier. He couldn't even handle a damn knife in a kitchen.

Brett quickly grabbed a towel to stop the bleeding. As he held the towel he saw a red stain slowly come through and spread and he thought about his friend Jin Lee and his dirty jokes and acne-scarred face. His Burmese parents wouldn't be having him over this holiday, and Brett briefly thought of the son Jin would never see. Brett quietly raged against the injustice. Jin had people who wanted him home, who cared about him. Brett had no one. He'd fooled himself into believing he had someone who cared. Someone to come home to. He'd fought to survive for nothing.

He watched a blood droplet fall and land on the cream tile floor and his mind turned to Roger Beal, who'd been found swinging in his girlfriend's basement. And for a moment he understood the quest for peace. The desire to escape oneself, one's mind. To escape the twin demons of anger and sorrow with no in between. Pain, pain, pain. Pain of loss, pain of betrayal, pain of guilt. Would the pain end? Should it?

"What did you do?" Miranda said when she saw him.

"It's nothing."

"You're bleeding all over my kitchen floor and you say it's nothing? Sit down."

He did so, his face burning from humiliation, but he kept his head high.

She looked at the wound. "You'll need stitches."

"I can handle it."

"What? You think you can stitch it up yourself with one hand?"

"Yes." He'd stitched up lots of wounds before, and he watched her, daring her to ask him to explain, but instead she shrugged and said, "Well, you're not going to. Come on."

***

He returned from having his hand stitched up at a near-by medical clinic, but quickly developed a fever. By the next day he was delirious. It had gotten infected and Miranda felt awful. She didn't know who she should call. If anything were to happen to him, it would be her fault, because of her silly lie. And in his delirium he spoke about his hates and fears and someone named Sarah. Was that someone to call?

Unfortunately, he didn't have a cell phone on him, which she found unusual for someone so young.

Fortunately, by the third day, the fever broke, but he was still weak.

"How long have I been like this?" Brett asked, his gaze drifting to the window where the moon shone bright outside.

"Two days."

He swore, then looked at her and apologized.

"That's okay, I'm your aunt, remember, not your mother."

He slowly sat up, making sure not to put any pressure on his wounded hand. "You're not even that."

"I'm just glad you're better. This is payback for letting me use you."

"No, I really—"

"That was a joke. Let's get you something to eat."

Moments later, Brett sat in the kitchen wearing an expensive maroon sweater Miranda had meant to give to John, feeling full after a meal she'd prepared. He looked around the kitchen at the frosted glass fronted cabinets and tea kettle in the shape of a hen. Miranda caught his look. "That was my father's favorite. Said it reminded him of my mother."

Brett wrapped his hand around the warm mug of spiced cider she'd prepared. "My mother was like this drink—soothing and sweet. You would have liked her."

"Wish I could have met her."

He took a sip of the cider then set it down. "Me too."

"What if…" Miranda stopped and bit her lip.

"What if what?" he urged her.

"It's a crazy idea, but just think about it. What if I were to meet them? What would breakfast have been like?"

Brett leaned back in his chair and shook his head. "It would have been crazy. Likely with my dad making obscure references about his favorite game of cricket and my mother asking me if I've had enough to eat while piling my plate with more food."

"Let me have them over for breakfast." Miranda held up a hand before he could speak. "I know it sounds crazy, but you pretended for me. Let me pretend for you. It's Christmas tomorrow and I'd really like to do this for you. What would you have liked to serve them?" She pulled out her cell phone to start a list.

"Are you serious?"

"Very. Come on. While you think of what you'd like to serve them let me go get my good dishes." She jumped up with the energy of a little girl getting ready to set up a tea party.

"But this is—"

"Never mind." She put her phone away. "I'll decide for you."

Chapter Seven

She'd done it again. Why couldn't he say no to her? Brett stared at the four place settings in wonder. Miranda almost made him really believe they were expecting guests. She'd given him one of her father's shirts and a pair of trousers to wear, but what amazed him more was that he was glad to have a reason to stay longer.

The cool morning rays of December splashed across the white plates and over the pan-fried jack, mackerel, scrambled eggs and papaya salad. Moments later, as she introduced herself and talked to the empty chairs in such a way that made it all seem real, he could see his parents. He could see the naughty twinkle in his father's eyes, the shy smile on his mother's face. Soon he was talking to them too and could imagine their laughter and feel their love. And for the first time in a long while, he felt at home, safe, wanted.

And he could imagine having a home of his own and a family. He turned towards the hallway. "Uh oh I hear the baby crying," he said.

Miranda's eyes widened. "Baby?"

The look of surprise on her face made him eager to continue the pretence. "Should I go check on her or—"

"Oh, no," she said, quickly catching on. "I'm sure your wife will have her quieted down soon and will join us."

His good humor fell. "No, I thought—"

"What?"

He stared at her, embarrassment seizing his heart. He thought what he shouldn't have. For a moment he'd imagined that they were…that she was…but that was wrong. She saw him as a substitute for her nephew, nothing more. And he felt ashamed of his feelings. He had so little he had to offer her. Plus, he knew she only saw the difference in their ages.

Miranda rested her hand on his arm and said, "I've been telling your parents what a good father you are."

He nearly lost it then. It was as if she'd uncovered a secret desire. He'd wanted to be the man his father had been to him. But not only had she said the words that hit him at his core, she'd touched him. He hadn't been touched like this in so long, too long and it sent a course of agonizing pleasure through him.

He didn't want to pretend any more. He didn't want to pretend to be her nephew, to pretend that his parents were alive, to pretend that he had a place to come home too. He had to end this.

He pulled his arm away. "I can't do this anymore."

Miranda blinked with concern. "I'm sorry I didn't mean—"

"It's all right. I'm just…I should go."

"What's the rush? I'd like to show you the store."

"No." He gathered up a plate and went into the kitchen.

"You're angry with me," she said, following him.

He set the plate down on the counter. "I'm not angry. I just…it's time for me to go."

"On Christmas Day?"

"Yes."

She rested her hands on her hips, staring at him for a long moment, then shrugged. "Okay." She left the kitchen.

He paused. Somehow he'd expected her to argue, to fight him. Or maybe he just wanted her to so she'd give him a reason to stay. He went back into the dining room where he found her cleaning up the table. "Miranda?"

"Yes?"

He stood in front of her. "I'm older than I look."

She grinned. "No, you're not."

He sighed. She was right.

"Besides, when you're in your twenties, it doesn't matter if you're twenty-four and she's twenty-five."

"I'm twenty-eight."

"Oh." She winked at him. "Then you are older than I thought. Anyway, there's no trouble if—"

"I'm not interested in Eva, I told you that before. I don't want to pretend anymore. I want to play the uncle."

She stared up at him, wide eyed. "You want to play my uncle?"

"No, that's not what I meant. I mean, I want you to play the aunt and I play the uncle."

Miranda shook her head then gathered up more plates and headed for the kitchen. "Perhaps we should stop playing altogether."

He blocked her path. "Only if we can start being real?"

"Real?"

He bit his lip then took a deep breath, holding her gaze even though it scared him. "Please tell me you feel it too."

Miranda took a hasty step back then set the plates on the table with a clatter. "Of course I feel it," she admitted, sounding breathless. "But it's just the season and we're both sad and lonely and happen to find—"

"Love?"

"Each other."

"Isn't that the same thing?"

"No."

With his good hand, he reached out and clasped her hand in his. "Yes, it is. We both know this feels right."

"Who's Sarah?"

He stiffened. "What?"

"You said her name over and over again when—"

"She's my past. She's…not part of my life right now. You don't have to worry about anybody else." Brett clasped her hand tighter, feeling her hesitation and fear. "I know it seems fast and I know it's sudden and I don't understand it all myself. But I do know that I want you to be a part of my life and I'll do whatever it takes to make that happen. I don't mind moving here and working in your store. Just until I get settled and—"

Miranda looked down at their joined hands. "This is crazy."

"No crazier than hosting my dead parents for breakfast."

"Well, when you say it like that," she began to say, but he stopped her words with a kiss. And soon no words were needed. When they finally drew apart, Miranda stared up at him in wonder. Was this really happening? She searched his face, seeing that the cynicism had gone from his eyes and voice, but there was still something a little sad in his expression. Something she couldn't understand.

"What do I have to do to get you to smile?" she asked.

He blinked, confused. "Why do I need to smile?"

"I don't know. So that I can know you're truly happy."

His brows shot up. "I don't look happy?"

"No."

"But I am," he said with feeling, gathering her close. "More than I can say," he said then kissed her again, determined to make her believe him.

They spent Christmas Day in a hazy, all-consuming joy. They went to the movies to watch the latest action film, Brett holding Miranda's hand every time she jumped in fright, or stroking her hair when she buried her face in his chest. Later, she showed him around the town and took him to her greatest pride—Simmonds Hardware. There, as she showed him around the building, where he saw a picture of her father as a young man, and they talked about the people they missed. The ones who never seemed far from their thoughts, but whose memory no longer caused them pain. That evening they shared their hopes and dreams for the future, falling asleep on the couch amidst the glow of fading firelight.

Miranda woke up before Brett and snuck into the kitchen, hoping to surprise him with breakfast. She had his tray made when someone knocked on the door. She rested the tray in the foyer and answered.

"We just got back," Eva said. "I wanted to see if you were okay and wanted to come over for—" She paused when her gaze fell on the tray. "What is that?" She didn't give Miranda a chance to respond. She pushed her way inside. "Is he still here? And he's making you wait on him hand and foot?"

"He's not making me do anything. We—"

Eva grabbed the tray. "He's already making himself king of the castle." She headed to the stairs.

"He's not there, he's in the living room, but—"

"But nothing. I might as well say 'hi' to him. You look as if you haven't slept."

Fortunately, Brett was awake when Eva stormed into the room; he'd heard her voice and then her pounding footsteps. He silently swore. She certainly wasn't the first face he wanted to see in the morning. He stood up and reached out to grab the tray, hoping he could balance it with one hand.

She set the tray down. "What did you do to your hand?"

"The moment it becomes any of your business I'll let you know."

Her lip became a straight line. "Now listen here—"

"It's Boxing Day, but not the type that you think," Miranda said, trying for humor. "Let's not—"

"I didn't expect you to still be here," Eva said, ignoring her. "But I'm glad you are. Because you don't fool me."

Brett sat down. "Fine, but first let me tell you—"

Eva sat cross from him, leaning forward as if she were in the middle of a tough negotiation. "I don't care what you have to say. Find someone else to live off of. Find some poor girl with a place of her own where you can move into. You may not remember, but I won't forget all the pain you've caused your aunt over the years. But if you do the right thing, I'll salute you on the way out."

"Eva, that's enough," Miranda said. "He doesn't deserve that."

"You're just blind because he's family."

"I'm not blind. I know that John is all that you've said. Unfortunately," she looked at Brett and offered him a wink. "Or perhaps fortunately, he's not him."

"What?"

"He was helping me save face. His name is Brett Greenwood."

Eva's eyes widened and she leaped to her feet. "What!"

"We both know—"

"That this is insane?" Eva finished, her voice near a shriek. "Ms. Miranda, you don't know what you're doing. You asked a perfect stranger into your home just so you could fool us?"

"He's not really a stranger. My father knew his father."

"So what?" Eva folded her arms and looked at Brett. "So what are your plans?"

"We plan to build a future together," Miranda said.

But Eva kept her gaze on Brett as if Miranda hadn't spoken. "Are you planning on moving into this lovely house and then working for her? That would be real cozy for you, wouldn't it? You wouldn't have to work hard at all."

"Eva, what we decide is none of your business."

Eva continued to keep her gaze on Brett. "I know it's a new age, but shouldn't a man provide something besides a dic—"

"Eva, I won't ask you again. He's a guest in my home and that's enough."

Eva spun towards her. "You're selling yourself short. You let John treat you like dirt and you'll let this man do it too. Aren't you tired of people feeling sorry for you?"

"Yes, but only because people feel sorry for me for the wrong reasons. They're sorry I'm not married or don't have kids. But I loved the life I made with my father and the adventures we had together. I don't regret helping my sister and nephew when they needed me. And I don't regret letting myself fall in love, even though I don't know the future."

"You're always taking care of others. When are you going to find a man who will take care of you?"

"She's met him," Brett said, standing and moving to Miranda's side. "I may not have much now, but I will."

"'Will' is a mighty long ways off from 'now,'" Eva said with a sneer. "Men like you are all talk. I met you in school, I see you in clubs, I see you at work. Opportunists who find lonely women—"

"Just go," Miranda said, surprised by the ugliness in Eva's tone. Eyes she'd once seen as so caring now frightened her, and the pity she'd feared to see had turned to disgust. "Before you say something that will end our friendship for good."

Eva spun around and walked away.

Chapter Eight

"We have to get rid of him," Eva said, after she'd told her mother about her conversation with Miranda. They both sat in their living room while her mother put aside the gift items they knew they'd never use.

"Why don't you leave the poor woman alone?"

"She doesn't know what she's doing."

"She's older than you are and has managed her life just fine," Mary said.

"You're the one who thought she was daft."

"I did, but maybe she knows something we don't."

"What could that be?"

"What love at first sight is."

Eva rolled her eyes. "That's ridiculous. She's being naïve and so are you. I know more about men my age than she does. She doesn't know what men can be like."

"You sound jealous."

"Me?" Eva rested a hand on her chest, wounded. "Jealous of her?"

"No, of him. Do you feel as if he's taking your place?"

"That's outrageous. I—"

Mary sent her daughter a level look. "Then leave her alone and stop worrying about things that have nothing to do with you."

"I know what men like him can be like. They see a woman with a fine house and good job and lonely bed and think they can fill it."

"And if she wants him to, is that your business?"

"She deserves better." Eva shook her head. "I can't believe—"

"If you'd stop talking, you'd open your eyes, pet."

"What?"

"Can't you recognize when you're in the presence of true love?" She smiled at her daughter's shocked expression. "I know that sounds odd coming from me, but it's true. I knew the first moment I saw him that he wasn't John."

"Yes, I felt it too because he's a fraud."

"No, because I saw a young man falling in love when he didn't expect to. Not even Miranda noticed how his gaze followed her. I'm glad they found each other." She stood. "So you leave them be," she said, then went upstairs.

True love? Eva looked out the window and stared at Miranda's house across the street, her mouth a straight line. "Sorry Mum, I can't."

Chapter Nine

Somehow she knew he'd disappear from her life. She'd remembered their last conversation before he'd gone to take a shower.

"She's right," Brett said, taking a seat on the couch, staring at the breakfast that had gone cold. "I don't have anything to offer you right now and—"

Miranda sat beside him, taking his hand. "That's okay."

He shook his head. "No, it's not okay. What would your father think of a man like me? Moving in, having you pay my wages. It doesn't look right. I should at least be making my own way."

"I need some help at the store and I could charge you room and board. How does that sound?"

He sighed. "Do you mind if I take a shower?"

"No, but a bath may be better. You don't want to get your hand wet."

"I'll wrap it tight," he said, then disappeared upstairs. She didn't follow him, giving him the space he needed.

She didn't know when he left. She'd been in the kitchen and hadn't heard his footsteps or the front door open and close, but when she'd gone upstairs, she found the door to his room open and the place empty.

Her heart cracked and bled. She'd lost him. A wonderful dream had ended. She knew one day he would leave, but she hadn't expected it to be without a goodbye. She blinked back tears, then quickly brushed them away when she heard the doorbell.

She opened the door and saw Eva with a plate of cookies. "It's a peace offering." She cleared her throat. "To both of you."

"He's gone," Miranda said with a sigh.

"Did he…?"

"He didn't say anything. He just left." She flashed a sad smile. "And there's no reason to pretend you aren't glad."

"That's not true. I was just worried about you. I didn't expect, I mean…I'm sorry."

"Don't be. I'll make some tea," Miranda said, heading towards the kitchen. "I'll meet you in the sitting room."

Eva slowly walked into the sitting room, stunned. Her wish had come true. He'd shown his true colors early. She'd gotten rid of him. She'd known he was no good, and now Miranda would see it. She hoped never to be as silly and romantic as her mother when she got older. *True love?* What crap. She sat down then saw a note on the coffee table. She picked it up.

"Darling Miranda, goodbyes are hard for me to say. I don't want to put pressure on you. I want to give you space to think about this…about us. I do love you, but if you don't feel the same, I understand. I'm taking the four o'clock bus back to New Jersey. If you

love me at all, and want to be my bride, just wave to me and I'll know your answer. Brett"

He'd left a letter. Eva jumped to her feet, thinking of Miranda's sad smile. Her friend needed to see this. To see how he felt about her. Eva took a step in the direction of the kitchen, then stopped. But what if it was just all words? How much of it was true? That grim, arrogant bastard had no right to live off of Miranda. Eva glanced at her watch. It was two o'clock. She heard Miranda's footsteps and crumpled the note in her fist before shoving it in her coat pocket. She was doing it for Miranda's own good.

"So I guess he's gone for good?" Eva asked, knowing the answer but wanting to hear it confirmed.

"Yes. He's moving on with his life."

"And so can you," Eva said, fighting hard to stop a smile.

Chapter Ten

Leaving had been hard, but he had no choice. Miranda was his weakness and she'd make him stay. But he had to do more. He had to make good, he had to be in a position to help provide. Eva's words sounded so much like something Sarah would say. That's why she'd chosen another man. Because he had nothing to offer. Could he blame her? He couldn't imagine facing Miranda's father or even his own with no prospects. How could he provide or protect her?

Brett paced inside the bus depot. He'd pack up his life in New Jersey then find a place and work in Hamsford. Now he had a mission. A purpose. And it felt good. He had a place to come back to and he hoped a woman waiting. He'd hoped she'd have come early to see him with her answer. He'd promised not to bother her, but the tension was killing him. Maybe she didn't really feel the way he did. Maybe it had all been just a dream. A holiday dream. Maybe he couldn't extend it.

He bit his lip. He'd been wrong about Sarah. Was he wrong about Miranda too?

No, he couldn't believe that. He glanced at his watch. She'd come.

*****

Just one more hour and he'd be gone for good, Eva thought as she flipped through the mail, Brett's note still crumpled up in her jean's pocket. She'd thought of throwing it away, but she couldn't risk anyone finding it. Their shredder was broken and if her mother saw her burning something she'd get suspicious. She'd get rid of it later, when that man was completely out of town.

"Why do you keep looking at the clock?" Mary asked, sitting down in front of Eva at the kitchen table.

"No reason…it's just…uh the mail carrier was late today."

Mary only nodded, sensing something was wrong, but not knowing what.

*****

Miranda sat in her living room and turned on her laptop to work on some accounts when she noticed a file was already opened.

Darling Miranda…

Brett had written her a note? When? Her heart raced as she read it. Why hadn't he left it out for her to see? Had he changed his mind? Had he meant to delete it? Should she pretend she hadn't seen it?

She closed the laptop and stood up. No, she couldn't. She'd find out the answer from him. She glanced at the clock. It was three-forty. She had twenty minutes to get to the bus depot.

She sped to the bus depot and jumped out of her car just as the bus was pulling away. She ran and waved her arms hoping he'd notice her, although she couldn't see him. She shouted his name, hoping he could hear her over the noise of the bus engine. She was about to give up when his face appeared in the window.

At first she wasn't sure it was him. His smile was so big it transformed his face. Tears of joy touched her eyes as she soaked in the sight of his happiness. She blew him a kiss. He pretended to grab it then hold it to his heart and then he was gone, leaving her with an image she'd keep in her mind until she saw him again.

Epilogue

A year later

With the fire crackling, they decorated their freshly picked Christmas tree, Afro-Brazilian music, the kind his father loved to listen to, playing in the background. There was still gossip in Hamsford about their small, hasty wedding and Miranda's 'young man.' "You know what he *really* married her for," some busybodies liked to say when they spotted the pair in the marketplace. But neither cared. Brett had already proven his worth with the employees of Simmonds Hardware and had doubled the profits within months. And as they celebrated their first Christmas together as a married couple, they felt as if they'd never been strangers.

"You're lucky I found the note on my laptop," Miranda said, placing a star ornament on the tree.

Brett adjusted a light and frowned. "I didn't leave a note on your laptop."

"Yes, you did. I read it and that's how I was able to see you before you left."

He shook his head. "But I didn't type anything. I hand-wrote it and left it on the coffee table."

"I never saw a written note." She grabbed her laptop, which had been on the coffee table, and opened the file she'd never delete. "You didn't write this?" she asked, showing the screen.

"Those are my words, but I didn't type it."

"That's strange," Miranda said, taking a seat.

He sat beside her. "Could you see me typing with one hand?"

"No, but that's so odd. I—" She stopped when the file suddenly disappeared and the image of a cocoa colored man with a white beard appeared on the screen.

Brett pointed to the picture, amazed. "That's him! That's the man who told me to come to Hamsford."

Miranda's mouth fell open. "What?"

"I should thank him for changing my life. I met him at the bus depot in New Jersey last year."

"You couldn't have," Miranda said, stumbling over the words. "Are you sure it was him?"

"Positive. Why do you doubt me?"

"Because that's my father."

Brett met her eyes, remembering the man's soft voice and warm presence. And then he thought about the day when they pretended that his parents had come to visit and how real it had all felt. Because it had been. Their spirits had joined them, and he'd never truly been alone. "He brought me to you."

"Well," Miranda said with a smile. "I told you my father always liked fixing things."

And then her husband kissed her smile away, and they were two broken hearts fully mended.

A Cup of Cheer

"No, no, no! I won't do it even for you."

"It's the holidays, Alyson. The least we can do as neighbors is spread good cheer."

"So you want me to give my delicious spiced cider to Scrooge next door?"

Of course his real name isn't Scrooge. It's Gareth LeBlanc owner of the second hand bookstore (creatively called Second Hand Books). Although the way he fussed over the books you'd think they were antiques instead of smelly old paperbacks and well worn hardbacks. I've only spoken to him a few times (when I wave 'hello', he just nods) and I can honestly say that I've only heard five sentences come out of his mouth. The only thing me or anyone else knows, was posted in a small write up in the weekly Community News: He was born in Dominica, the son of an English father and Dominican mother, and has travelled extensively.

When he first moved in, I sent him a box of cookies to welcome him to the neighborhood. I knew that he lived in the apartment above his shop, as I did, and I'd hoped to be as friendly with him as I had been with the previous residents—two elderly sisters from Trinidad who said my coconut cookies were divine. He didn't say they were divine, he didn't even say they were nice. He just returned an empty tin with a sticky note that said 'Thanks'. That's it, nothing more…just 'Thanks'.

It took me weeks before I could stomach the thought of stopping by his shop. I finally decided to visit in order to see the type of cookbooks he had. I have to give him credit, he had a pretty good selection. So every few weeks I'd stop by and buy a few. I was buying two when I noticed this beautifully bound book from the early twentieth century called *Amelia Armand's Complete Book of Spices*. It was encased in the curio behind his head. I was certain it would be expensive, but I was willing to pay the price.

I am a culinary historian and when I'm not in my store selling traditional and rustic crafts and recipe books, I recreate authentic dishes for functions at the Historical Society. A book like that would have been perfect for my collection.

"How much is that book behind you?" I asked after purchasing several items. He adjusted the rim of his baseball cap. He always wore a baseball cap (perhaps he was going bald) and a tie that never matched his shirt (and color blind?)— orange against a tan shirt.

He didn't even turn around to see what I was referring to. "It's not for sale," he said in a cutting deep voice that could cause one to have goose bumps, if one liked the resonant sound of low baritones. I haven't stepped foot in that bookstore since. I'd rather drop my money in a sewer than fatten his bank account again.

"Since you're so desperate to spread holiday cheer why don't you do it?" I asked Cora.

"Because I didn't make the cider and it is better coming from you. You have that cheery, friendly aura about you."

"You mean jolly, don't you?"

She made a face, but wisely didn't reply. I'm not fat, but I'm not slim either. Not like Cora who has a nice slender build which she further accentuated by wearing tight suede trousers, a pink cashmere blouse and black boots with heels that could cause the sidewalk to crack. But I didn't envy her, I had inherited my stout full-figure like all the women in my family and was curvy in all the right places. My mother who had been born in Venezuela, of Trinidadian parents and Barbadian grandparents had made sure, while I was growing up, that I would be proud of my figure. I preferred my loose fitting cotton tops and trousers and comfortable walking shoes. Customers said I made them feel at home and that feeling was always good for business.

"Besides, it's slick and icy outside," she complained. "You wouldn't want me to trip, would you?" She wiggled her high heeled boot.

"It would serve you right."

"But what would you do without me?"

I scowled. She was right; her business acumen had helped turn my small shop into an international destination. I was getting mail orders from as far away as Dubai.

"He's not married, you know."

I rolled my eyes. "Yes, I heard Dracula is single too."

She sent me a look; I ignored her. Ever since I hired her as my assistant five years ago she's been trying to match me up. It's not that I don't like men. I do. Just not modern men. You know: the modern man who won't hold the door open for you, but instead will let it slam in your face; the modern man who expects you to pay for dinner while he pays for dessert; the modern man who thinks the question "Would you like to come inside?" means you.

I wanted something more. I wanted romance. Grand gestures like a carriage ride on a snowy day, or holding out my chair and remembering to walk on the outside of the pavement so that passing cars wouldn't splash me. Or even calling me by my name instead of 'honey' or babe' or confusing me for another woman (a long story). But I'd given up on romance years ago. Modern men didn't do grand gestures. They didn't even do small ones.

"Look, it's starting to snow," Cora said, glancing out the shop window. "How can you not be friendly at a time like this when everything looks white and fresh?" She shoved the thermos filled with hot cinnamon-nutmeg cider into my chest. "Go on and spread some holiday cheer."

"He'll probably bite my head off again," I mumbled slipping into my coat and hat.

"He's just a man, Alyson. Not the big bad wolf."

I made a face and wrapped a scarf around my neck.

***

The wind nearly knocked me back into the shop. A freezing blast stung my cheeks while a stream of cold tears fell from my eyes. He's not worth this. I turned around ready to go back in my store. Cora blocked the doorway and mouthed 'Go.' I briefly wondered how many homicides occurred during the holiday season then spun around and hurried next door.

The bell chimed above my head as I entered the shop. It was quiet with only a few customers rummaging through books on the shelves. I stomped my snow-covered boots on the rug and glanced towards the counter, which was conveniently empty. Perhaps he was out back somewhere polishing one of his beloved books. I could leave the cider on his desk with the added benefit of not having to see him. Great! I smiled in triumph, took one of his business cards and scribbled 'Happy Holidays' on the back.

Once finished I looked up and saw it: The book. I glanced side to side to make sure no one was watching then I lifted myself on the counter, leaned closer and squinted, hoping I could tell whether the book was really old or just an imitation. By looking at the paper texture and type it looked like the real thing. My mind raced with all the possible recipes hidden inside.

"It's not for sale."

I fell back and stumbled before regaining my footing. I stared at him. Or rather at his chest, since that was the first thing I saw. Today he wore a red shirt and green tie—at least he looked festive. Although I doubt that was his intention, he didn't seem the festive sort. I finally raised my gaze to his face. As usual he wore his baseball cap low, shading his eyes. I was glad since I didn't care to read their expression. "You know I could offer you a lot of money…"

"It's still not for sale," he repeated in that same deep baritone.

"Then why do you have it there?"

"Because I like it there." He abruptly turned and went behind the counter. "But you're right, I should make things clear." He quickly wrote a sign that said 'Display Only' then taped it up. He then turned to me. "Better?"

I frowned, trying my best to look confused. "Does that mean it's not for sale?"

He blinked looking bored. "Did you want something?"

I didn't think he would have appreciated hot spiced cider over his head so I shoved the thermos into his chest, which was surprisingly harder than I thought it would be. Weren't dusty bookworms supposed to be a little soft around the middle? "This is for you."

He frowned and looked down at the thermos. "What is it?"

"It's poison."

He glanced up quickly. His surprise gave me a chance to look at his eyes, which were big, brown and oddly innocent.

No one with eyes like those could be all bad. "I was hoping to kill you off so I could steal the book."

The corner of his mouth kicked up as he twisted the lid and took a sniff. "Smells like hot cider."

"Spiced cinnamon-nutmeg cider if you want to be specific."

He poured himself a cup then took a sip, nodded as though in approval then looked at me with a playful glare that said a lot more. "It's still not for sale."

I shrugged, feigning defeat. "I know." I took a step back, suddenly feeling both restless and giddy at the same time. I knew it was time to leave. "Well, Happy Holidays." I turned and left before he could say anything more.

***

He returned the thermos the next day, or rather had it delivered. I had been working on our website when Cora came into the office. She held the thermos against her and said in a loud stage whisper. "It's from him."

"Him who?"

"Scrooge."

I pretended not to care, though I felt my face grow warm. "So? Set it in the kitchen."

She waved a piece of paper. "He sent you a note."

I took the envelope (Cora said I snatched it, but she tends to be dramatic). It was real parchment paper with my name scribbled across in his broad handwriting. For a moment I pictured him sitting at an old oak desk under a low hanging lamp, while a stripped cat sat on his shoulder, lazily waving its tail (Gareth didn't have a cat, but I liked the image). I could hear the smooth movement as his pen glided across the paper. Once he was finished, he carefully folded the note and placed it inside the envelope then slowly licked and sealed it closed. I brought the envelope to my nose. Did his scent cling to it or was it just my imagination?

Cora's voice cut into my daydream. "Aren't you going to open it?"

I blinked, shocked out of my fantasy, then ripped open the letter.

Dear Ms. Haywood:

There are few things in life that can be described as perfect: A starry sky, a new dawn and your spiced cinnamon-nutmeg cider. May I request another? Bring it by tomorrow. I will pay accordingly.

Sincerely,

Gareth LeBlanc

"What does it say?" Cora asked trying to peer over my shoulder. I handed her the note. She read it and frowned. "Well it certainly isn't poetry. Dear Ms. Haywood? It sounds so cold and formal. So what are you going to do?"

I wasn't sure, but I planned to think of something.

***

The following day brought sunshine, the sound of birds chirping, the distant ring of a Salvation Army Santa, and the steady drip of snow melting on the rooftop. I took my basket and headed next door. The sign on the door said 'Closed' and I was about to ring the bell when I looked through the store's glass front door and saw Gareth wearing a faded brown corduroy jacket and baseball cap talking to a woman in a long white cashmere coat. It didn't look like a happy conversation. I started to turn when the woman raced out the door in tears. Gareth followed, but didn't call out her name or tell her to stop. He just watched her go. It was obviously a lover's quarrel and not something I wanted to be a part of. I took two quick steps back hoping I could escape before he saw me.

"I hate the holidays," he mumbled then turned before I was a safe distance away. He stared at me surprised. "What do you want?"

I took another quick step back towards the freedom and safety of my store. "Nothing. I just—"

He held open the door. "Come on in."

I swallowed, wondering if I should refuse him, but decided to take the risk and go inside suddenly aware that it was the first time I'd ever been alone with him.

"I could come back another time."

He shook his head. "Doesn't matter. I shouldn't even be here." He gestured to the books around him. "All of this was my brother's idea. I was going to help him. He was the one with the pleasing personality and charm. He was going to be the one upfront dealing with the customers and I'd be in the back handling the accounting and other mundane business. He was so happy when he found this building and we signed the lease." Gareth angrily adjusted his cap. "After he died I should have just let everything go, but I couldn't. I wanted to fulfill this dream for him, but I'm all wrong. I'm not good with people—I prefer eReaders and computers and computer games. But the strange thing is that business is booming but Jani wants me to leave."

"Jani?"

"My ex-girlfriend, she's the one who just left. She wants me to give it up and return to my old job, but I can't." He stared at me and shook his head amazed. "I don't know why I'm telling you all this."

I smiled. "I'm easy to talk to."

He didn't return my smile, but his face softened. "You would have liked Rupert."

"His brother's not too bad either."

Gareth's gaze fell and I winced, knowing that's probably not something he wanted to hear. Now was not the time to flirt.

"The holidays can be hard for anyone," I said hoping to cover my gaffe and find a way to comfort him. "Especially when you've lost someone you care about, but I'm sure he'd want you to be happy."

Gareth let out a tired sigh. "He would and I'm letting him down. I mean what right do I have to be happy living his dream?"

"People don't own dreams and from what you've told me, it was a dream you had together. I bet you his spirit is here with you cheering you on."

Gareth sent me a long look I couldn't read. I licked my lip wondering if he was going to tell me to leave or mind my own business. Instead he spun around, said "Give me a minute" then disappeared upstairs.

I didn't move. I thought about leaving, but I was too curious to do so. I thought about his brother. I thought about how lonely it must be for Gareth to be here in this empty shop.

"Okay, come up," he called from above.

I hesitated then walked up the stairs to the main landing then into a nice living area. The heat of a crackling fire met me first, followed by the sounds of carols drifting from the radio. A tiny Christmas tree sat on the windowsill with a crooked star on top. I straightened it, crooked things annoy me.

"I thought you hated Christmas," I called out to him.

"I changed my mind," he said from another room. "Take a seat."

"No, I have something to show you first."

"More cider?"

"No. I'm going to show you how to make your own."

He came out of the other room and stared at me surprised. I stared back equally stunned. He wasn't wearing his hat. Although everything else was the same—he wore a dreadful checkered maroon tie with a striped shirt—I felt as though I'd met him half dressed, exposed. I'd uncovered his secret. He wasn't going bald, he had cropped black hair, and the most expressive deep brown eyes I'd ever seen. Every emotion he felt flashed in them; I could see they were his most vulnerable feature. And something in their expression seemed to ignite something inside me. Something I'd ignored for a long time. I'd buried myself in history and the past so that I wouldn't be vulnerable in the present, but at that moment Gareth had shown me that people hadn't changed that much. Their hopes, fears and dreams remained the same.

His eyes changed from surprised to weariness. "You're going to teach me?"

"Yes."

He flashed one of his odd little half smiles then disappeared into the room again, he reappeared with his baseball cap.

I took it off. "You look better without it."

He put it back on. "It brings me luck."

"You don't need luck."

He grabbed my hand before I could take it off. "How about courage then? It's a crutch, but it works for me.

Superman has his cape, Wolverine has his claws and I have my cap, okay?"

"Fine," I said, though I wondered how I could convince him otherwise. He really did have very nice eyes.

Gareth showed me the kitchen and we both went inside. Making cinnamon-nutmeg cider only takes ten minutes. Somehow I made it last an hour; neither of us noticed the time. As the cider simmered on the stove the smell of cloves, nutmeg, apples, cinnamon, and sweet brown sugar permeated the air.

When the cider was done we sat in his alcove that looked down into the quiet bookshop and drank in peaceful silence.

"Books make sorry companions after awhile," he finally said.

Both pain and resignation seeped behind his simple words. "History can lose its appeal too," I said.

We slipped into silence again then he abruptly stood, picked up a book from off the shelf and handed it to me.

I stared at him stunned. "Amelia Armand's Complete Book of Spices? You can't give this to me."

He took a sip of his cider and sent me a full grin. "I'm not. It's still not for sale." He tipped his hat back a bit. "But you can come by and use it anytime."

I set the book down—at that moment I didn't care what was inside—instead I took his cap off and placed it on my head. It was a bold move to make, but I was a modern woman and decided to take the risk.

And he being a modern man…well let's just say I didn't open *Amelia Armand's Complete Book of Spices* until late New Years and I didn't mind a bit.

New Year's Surprise

Divorce. Millions of people did it, but that didn't stop Pam Rubin from feeling alone. The man she'd thought she'd spend the rest of her life with would no longer be part of it. She knew it was the right decision. They'd been separated six months now, but they'd been emotionally apart longer than that. Living in the same house but living separate lives. She still didn't know where things had gone wrong. When had they stopped loving each other? When had simple disagreements become a war?

But she didn't want to think about that now. She had come to her sister's New Year's Eve party, instead of staying home with her dog and watching the ball drop on TV, to cast aside the loneliness that seemed to stick to her skin like masking tape. No, tonight was a promise of new things and a new future. Pam stood with a glass in her hand, a fake look of joy on her face, feeling out of step with all the happy couples that surrounded her. It was strange how, as her marriage crumbled, that's all she started to see: happy newlyweds, happy parents with their children, happy older couples celebrating decades together. She and Jerrod had only made five years and there had been no children, but not for lack of trying.

Pam leaned against the balcony railing. The stars shone bright above her. She preferred looking at them instead of all the ruby earrings and emerald necklaces that graced the ladies inside the house. The dazzling gold wedding bands and diamond engagement rings seemed to sparkle under the lights, catching her eye where ever she turned. She glanced down at her now bare hand, her loneliness making her feel invisible.

"There you are!" her sister, Darlene, said coming up to her, wearing a slinky sequence dress her own wedding ring twinkling under the Japanese lanterns that decorated the balcony. She was four years older with bouncing black curls and light brown eyes. She was usually considered the prettier of the two sisters because of her vivacious personality and engaging smile that some said was as sweet as grata cake. "I was looking all over for you! What are you doing standing out here by yourself? You're a single woman now, you should be living it up."

Pam shook her head, a strand of hair falling from her French twist. She narrowed her dark brown eyes. "I'm not single yet."

"You will be. You might as well start the New Year with a new man. Out with the old and in with the new."

Pam knew her sister didn't understand how raw she still felt. She didn't want a new man when she still couldn't understand how she'd lost the old one. "I'm not ready yet."

"It's been six months. Admit that it's over between you. You told me how happy you've been with him away. It may feel awkward, but it's time to get into the dating pool again."

"I don't know how to swim," Pam said in a dry attempt at humor.

"Just stay in the shallow end. Lucky for you your big sister is here to help. I have someone who is perfect for you."

Pam inwardly groaned. "I've given up on men."

Darlene opened her mouth then closed it then opened it again and said in a low, cautious tone. "So you're into women now?"

Pam laughed. "I'm not into anyone now. I am just through with relationships. I'm happier by myself."

Darlene visibly relaxed and rested a hand on her sister's shoulder, her voice eager. "You're going to like him. He—"

"I don't care."

"You will care when you meet him. His parents are from Barbados and he has a doctorate in..." She frowned. "I forgot," she said with a careless wave of her hand. "But he's smart and I know that you like that in a man."

Pam sent her sister a look. He sounded just like her soon-to-be-ex. "I didn't come here to meet anybody."

Her sister clasped her hands together as if ready to beg. "If you'll just meet him, I will leave you alone. I promise. I really want you to meet him."

Pam set her wine glass down. It wasn't like her sister to be so insistent. Since she'd agreed to come to the party she might as well try to be sociable. "Okay. Let me go freshen up."

"Yes," Darlene said as Pam turned to leave. "Don't forget to add more lipstick, take the shine off your nose and for goodness sake consider letting your hair down."

***

Pam stared at her reflection in the bathroom mirror, feeling as though she was staring at a stranger. Who was that woman with hollow eyes and pinched lips? When was the last time she'd smiled? She shouldn't have come. She didn't want to meet anyone. She wasn't ready to. She knew her sister meant well but that didn't make her feel better. She had to leave. She would grab her coat and go. Satisfied with her plan, Pam left the bathroom and headed for the room where all the coats were piled up on a bed. She was halfway down the hall ready to go upstairs when she saw her sister standing next to a man. He looked very genial and attractive, but she didn't want to meet him. She prayed her sister didn't turn and see her. She wanted to escape. Pam frantically glanced around then darted into the first door she saw: The closet. She knew it was cowardly but she didn't care.

The closet had a familiar pleasant smell of lemon and spice, relaxing her a bit. She leaned against the wall, letting out a startled screech when it moved.

"Shh, you'll give us away," a deep voice said.

"What are you doing in here?" she demanded in a loud whisper.

"I wanted to be alone."

"Then why did you come to a party?"

"I was invited," he said. "But now I'm not sure that was a good idea."

"Then why don't you go home?" Pam asked annoyed by the tremor in her voice. She was used to being calm in any situation but this man had unnerved her.

"Because I just got here."

"You're being ridiculous."

"I could say the same about you," he said with laughter in his voice.

He was right. His reasons for hiding were eerily similar to hers. She should follow her own advice and just leave. "I'm sorry," she said then became quiet when she heard people passing by. "You just scared the living daylights out of me. I'm hiding from my sister." Pam folded her arms then looked up at the figure next to her. She was unable to see his face clearly except for some light that seeped through the slits in the closet door. It highlighted a forehead, nose and mouth. She took several deep breaths and soon her heartbeat returned to normal. She should be panicked and waited for anxiety to seize her, but oddly it didn't. After the initial shock of surprise she felt strangely resigned by the situation. At least she knew where the lemon and spice scent came from. Every time he moved the scent seemed to embrace her and reminded her of happier times.

"So why are you hiding from your sister?" he asked.

Pam briefly shut her eyes. She hadn't expected the question. She didn't want him to care. Wasn't sure she could trust him. But somehow the darkness was a comfort. What was it about the dark that made sharing seem safe? That made two people feel intimate? She didn't think too much about it. She was relieved to have the chance to speak to a man she'd never speak to again.

"She wants to fix me up with a man."

"Don't you like men?"

"I'm not very lucky with them."

"I don't believe that."

She sniffed. He would say that and eight years ago she would have believed him. She'd met her soon-to-be-ex at a party like this. But she'd been a different woman then. A woman with a promising future and bright ideas. She'd worn a blue velvet dress and spinning gold earrings. She'd just escaped the attention of two graduate students who'd bored her with their pretentiousness when a tall man stepped into her path and said, "A professor or a teacher?"

She looked at him startled. "What?"

He held out his arms to the side. "Do I look like a professor or a teacher?"

Pam surveyed his clothes and shook her head puzzled. He didn't look like either. He looked like a corporate raider. He wore all black, which only emphasized a large intimidating build. He had a carefully trimmed goatee, his black hair shone low, skin like molasses, feather-like long lashes and piercing brown eyes. "Does it matter?" she asked.

He let out a sigh. "Yes, I've got a job interview in a week and I really need to make the right impression. I've already had ten others with no results."

"Well, first you're too on the point?"

He frowned. "On the point?"

"Yes," she said with a light laugh. "I don't even know your name."

He held out his hand Jerrod Fuller."

"I'm Pam Rubin and I don't think you look like a teacher or professor. Anyone looking at you would see an ambitious young man who would take over their job one day."

He raised a dark eyebrow. "I'm ambitious."

"You don't have to wear it like a banner. You can go for business casual. Also, focus on the needs of the school. How you'll be a value to them."

Jerrod nodded. "I can do that. Are you free tomorrow?"

Pam paused. "For what?"

"For dinner. I'd like to get more of your advice."

"But I don't have much to say," Pam stuttered feeling her face grow warm.

A sly grin touched the corner of his mouth. "I'm sure you do and I'm prepared to listen to every word."

And he did. He just let her talk and his dark eyes watched her as if she were the most fascinating and beautiful woman in the world. And she in turn helped him soften his look so that he didn't appear so intimidating. Although he looked like the kind of man who'd likely have gotten into college on a sports scholarship he'd actually gotten a scholarship in science, played tennis and had a passion for abstract art. A week later he aced his interview. A week after that he was hired and a month later they were inseparable. Their first New Year's Eve together had been simple and beautiful. A quiet time at home with a bottle of champagne and a ring. He'd told her he wanted to spend every New Year with her and asked her to marry him. And she'd said yes. It had all seemed so perfect but she hadn't known that something would destroy that peace. That it had a name.

Fear. How come no one ever talked about how fear can enter a marriage? How it can erode trust and communication? How it can slowly eat away at what one has struggled to build? Pam still remembered her mother's sneer on the day of the rehearsal dinner. "He's just a teacher. He's got no money. There's no need to marry the bastard."

Pam gritted her teeth. "He's not a bastard."

"One day you'll think so."

"No, I won't. I love him."

"That will change."

Had it? Had it changed? The butterflies had gone and familiarity had taken away the rush of romantic surprise and the high of falling in love. But the sun was also familiar, however she never grew tired of its dancing rays. It had been the same with Jerrod except, unlike the sun, she'd started to worry that he wouldn't always be there. And one day she'd been right. She hadn't wanted to be her mother, but she'd taken her mother's bitterness and fear into the marriage. Their six months apart had taught her a lot about herself.

She used to watch Jerrod at a party with admiration so glad that he was hers. She didn't even know when her casual glances turned to suspicion. When she'd watch him with a woman with careful surveillance as though a police officer on the trail of a suspect. She would watch how he tilted his head, his eyes, his smile. She'd watch the woman too. Notice how she touched him, if it was a hand to his shoulder or his sleeve and she'd wondered what the gesture meant. She never confronted him because she knew what he would say. Her father had said the same. She just let her suspicions grow and her fears mingled with them until there was a wall around her heart. She knew he felt it too, but they never talked about it. Soon they never talked about anything not pay cuts, tight schedules or family illnesses and after their last attempt at having a child she knew there was nothing else to keep them together.

Pam sighed feeling the weight of her loss. She'd loved him. She'd thought he'd loved her. Where had it gone wrong? She angrily brushed away a clothes hanger, wishing she'd brought a glass of wine in the closet with her.

"I'm sure he has no problems with the ladies," Pam said sourly, wanting to take the focus off of her. "He never did."

"You never know."

She nodded. "You're right. I don't. I stopped knowing very much about him after awhile. Somehow we just stopped talking."

"Did you ever try to talk?"

"Yes, but it soon became too painful, especially when we couldn't have kids. I know how much he wants to be a father."

She heard him rub his hands together. "I doubt that's the only reason he married you."

"Well it seemed that's where everything fell apart."

"I bet there were other things. I mean my wife only cared about starting a family, but for me it was too stressful."

"You don't want kids?" she asked more sharply than she wanted to. "I mean it's okay if you don't," she added more softly not wanting him to stop talking.

"I did—do, but at the time my father was dying and I couldn't focus on anything else."

His words made her heart constrict with sorrow. "I'm sorry about your father."

He sighed. "He loved my wife. I'm glad he didn't see my marriage end."

"Did you love your wife?"

"Still do."

Her voice cracked with surprise and suspicion. "Really?"

"Yes, everyone keeps telling me to move on and I know I should, but something is holding me back and I think that's it."

"Sometimes our hearts mislead us."

He shook his head. "Not often, especially not mine."

Pam fell silent unable to believe his words. They sounded genuine, but if he really loved his wife why hadn't he fought to keep his marriage? She rubbed her forehead, wishing she could gather her warring thoughts, then let her hand fall. "If you could do it all again, what would you do?"

He was silent a long moment then said, "Apologize for not admitting how unhappy I was. I would have been more honest. You?"

"Same. I would have given him more space. I wanted him to talk to me and I think that just pushed him further away. I wanted him to turn to me. But he turned to someone else instead."

"Are you sure about that?"

"Positive."

"How?"

Pam shrugged feeling the wall around her heart starting to rebuild. "The usual," she said trying to sound casual although the memory of his deception pierced her. "Secret phone calls. Cryptic notes. Strange perfume on his clothes." She'd been taught by her twice divorced mother that if you didn't have a man's attention someone else did. Her father hadn't been true to any of his five wives. Now that he was older he was slowing down so wife number six may be lucky. Women found Jerrod attractive and he never had trouble getting noticed. She was attractive too, but she knew that wasn't enough to keep a man. Her mother had been beautiful and kept the house running while also working and that still hadn't made her father faithful. Without kids Pam couldn't think of anything to get Jerrod to stay.

"Did you tell him?"

"No," Pam said quickly. "I didn't want to know the details. I failed him. I didn't want to know about the woman who hadn't. I'd once been the most important woman in his life and then it ended. When a man cheats it's over."

"So if he'd told you why he cheated you wouldn't have forgiven him?"

"Sure I'd forgive him, but I couldn't trust him. If he's unhappy he deserves to leave. It's just a symptom. I'm sure he's happy with whoever he's with now."

"Trust is important."

"Yes."

"My wife never trusted me."

Pam paused surprised by his statement. She drummed her fingers against her thigh. "Did you give her a reason not to?"

"No. I could never do or say enough to make her believe in me. At first she did. She made me feel like the greatest man on the planet and then, after we married, that changed. I gave her gifts. I told her how much I loved her, but if I came home late or she saw me with a female colleague she'd assume the worse."

Pam released a tired sigh feeling suddenly worn. "I guess that's unfair."

"Yes. You can't have a relationship without trust."

"Hmm."

"But I lied. I did give my wife a reason not to trust me."

"I knew it," Pam said satisfied that he was just as she'd suspected him to be: A typical male. "What was it?"

"I kept a secret from her."

She bit her lip her heart picking up pace. "What?"

"After my father died I started thinking about my own morality. It can hit a man hard sometimes. I went to get checked and discovered I was genetically disposed to have the same condition that killed my father. I started to do lots of tests and even started therapy to deal with my fear."

"Why didn't you tell m—her? Why keep that a secret?"

"Because by that time she was so focused on having a family and not succeeding and I didn't want to feel as if I'd failed her on something else."

"But she would have been there for you. I know she didn't marry you just so you could be a father."

"It's broken up marriages before."

"But if you'd talked..." Pam let her words trail off. Obviously he hadn't trusted her.

He shifted, the sleeve of his shirt brushing hers, the lemon and spice sense embracing her again. "Too bad you never talked about it."

"Yes."

"I guess we both failed," he said.

Pam hugged herself, feeling the wall around her heart crumbling but terrified of being vulnerable again as she let hope seep in. "Think there's any way to fix it?"

"Maybe by remembering the good times. Where there any?"

Pam smiled. "Yes."

"Tell me."

"I used to love when he'd sing off key in the shower. He has a really good voice and knew his singing would always make me laugh and it did. He also used to have this strange way of knowing who was calling without looking at the caller ID. He'd be in the living room reading and the phone would ring and he'd say "Pick up it's your mother" or "Forget it, it's my sister." And more often than not he was right. I used to tease him that he was psychic. We loved going to concerts. Indoor, outdoor, bands, symphonies. Anything. He could always make the outing an adventure because he knew how to move in a crowd. In the early days I loved to listen to him talk about his students and he supported me while I got my Masters. Even when I felt like giving up he always believed in me."

"Sounds like good times."

Pam felt her heart lift. "They were." She hesitated then asked, "How about you?"

"My wife used to put lollipops in my briefcase with a note that said 'Have a sweet day.' She'd also coordinate the closet by color, matching shirts with ties, belts with pants, socks with shoes."

Pam groaned. "She sounds controlling."

He shook his head and laughed. "I liked it. I didn't have to think hard. If I grabbed a shirt I could see what tie could go with it. It made my morning easier and made me feel that she cared about me."

"She still doesn't sound like much fun."

"Maybe to some. I know with you having a husband who likes to go out and mingle and have different adventures you wouldn't understand how important it can be to have a place that's organized. Someone who is settled and grounded. I grew up around a lot of chaos and my wife helped me learn to live a different way. Just being with her was fun. We'd sit together and just talk or watch TV or play a video game, or tell corny jokes. I miss that. I miss her."

Pam blinked back tears. "I miss him too, but are memories really enough? I was so afraid of losing him that I pushed him away. I don't think I can fix that." It was too much. The man, the memories. Suddenly instead of feeling like a confessional the closet felt like a tomb. She couldn't breathe. She grabbed the door and opened it desperate to escape.

He grabbed her arm. "Pam wait."

She shook her head. "When I first heard your voice I nearly ran out."

"I'm glad you didn't," he said in a velvet whisper, tenderly turning her to face him.

She squeezed her eyes shut. She couldn't look at him. It had been so intimate in the closet and had felt safe, but now she felt exposed. She didn't want to look at him, but she knew she had to. She gathered her courage and faced him: The tall good looking man with skin like molasses and featherlike lashes who'd helped her sort through her mixed feelings. The man who had once asked her if he looked like a teacher or professor. The man who'd asked her to marry him on New Year's Eve.

"I want you back," Jerrod said.

"Why?" Pam said in a broken voice.

"I'm sorry I pulled away from you and kept secrets. I know it was wrong, but I want a second chance."

"Why?"

"I told. I love you."

"But I pushed you away with my suspicions and—"

"You made a mistake and I did too. That makes us human. And one thing I've learned about being human is that we can break, but we can also heal." His gaze fell. "When your sister invited me I wasn't going to come. I was angry, but somehow she convinced me." His gaze met and held hers. "I'm glad I did."

"But you ended up in the closet."

A sheepish grin touched his lips. "I know. When I saw you I couldn't face you so I hid. And the next thing I knew you were in here too."

"Hiding from my sister." Pam took his large hand and cradled it in hers. "I guess it's time we both stopped hiding."

"Yes."

She lightly brushed her thumb over the back of his hand. "My sister thought I should start the upcoming year with a new man."

Jerrod pulled her into the circle of his arms and he looked down at her as if she were the most fascinating and beautiful woman he knew. "I am a new man and I'm all yours, if you want me."

Pam cupped his face in her hands and kissed him. "I love you," she whispered against his lips, wanting him to know that she still thought he was the greatest man in the world. She gave her heart to him with complete trust, casting all fear away.

His lips met hers with a tender silent vow and at that moment their wounds began to heal. Neither noticed when the clock struck twelve.

Darlene saw them and raised a glass relieved that her plan had worked. "Happy New Year you two. May it be filled with many more wonderful surprises."

Something New

All Lewa Olunlade wanted for Thanksgiving was a turkey and her sister's husband. At thirty-four she dreaded going home for the traditional family gathering where people would laud her sister's excellent 'catch' and bemoan Lewa's single state. She could already imagine what "the Aunts" would say. Although not related by blood, Lewa called them her Aunts out of respect and cultural norm which acknowledged both their ages and that they were close family friends.

"You must stop being so picky," Aunty Elizabeth would say.

"I had two children by your age," Aunty Femi would add with a note of pride.

"The further you're past thirty, your chances of a good husband dwindle to nearly nothing."

"Unless you want a divorced man."

"And he'll probably have children."

"And who wants to raise someone else's children?" Aunty Elizabeth would say with a ring of superiority and distaste, having made herself an expert on men, marriage and childrearing. Although she'd twice had her face rearranged by her husband's fists, no one ever spoke about it because at least she was married and had two wonderful children. At sixty, she'd left her husband in Nigeria, who was now using his fists to beat his mistress and his four children by her, and she was finally free to use the power of being a married woman without having to deal with all the realities.

Aunty Femi had three children who basically tried to ignore her existence so she spent every holiday with the Olunlade family instead. None of her children felt it necessary to include her in their holiday gatherings since she was on the southern East Coast and they had all decided to settle in the northern region. They sent her money to assuage their guilt for their shoddy treatment of her and occasionally an email or a brief phone call, but little else. Lewa could guess that her children were likely embarrassed by their mother's loud coarse ways—her English was poor and her table manners worse. However, Lewa knew Aunty Femi had a good heart and could understand her parents' affection for her. Aunty Femi's marriage had been fine, she'd been a widow for ten years, but Lewa gave up trying to decipher what 'fine' meant although she had on a number of occasions asked Aunty Femi if she'd been happy. Aunty Femi would only reply that she'd been married and leave it at that.

Lewa understood the underlining truth behind every word and glance of the Aunts and her mother: It was better to have a husband—no matter how wretched— than no husband at all. It was a woman's fate. And she was arrogant and naive to expect any better.

"Caring for another man's children isn't so bad, if the woman isn't around," Aunty Femi would say to continue the conversation. She liked to talk and the topic of marriage and children made her feel smart.

"But then again, a woman isn't meant to be alone, so a divorced man is better than no man," Aunty Elizabeth would add and the Aunts would nod and continue to talk about her as if she wasn't there, because in a way she wasn't. A single woman in her family amounted to only half a woman. Not even a woman, half a person. Lewa could only hope that soon the talk would shift back to her sister, who'd been married three years but still hadn't had a child.

It had surprised everyone that by the end of the first year of marriage she hadn't introduced a new family member, preferably a boy, of course, but a girl would suit as well. After the first childless year, Lewa's sister, Arielle, had just laughed at the teasing, but Lewa could see the strain in her sister's eyes and plastered grin with each passing year.

Maybe this year she'd announce the news her family expected to hear. Lewa could imagine her sister and her husband, Stillman, making good parents. Stillman hit the marriage tri-fecta—family from the upper echelon of Nigerian society, Oxford educated with another degree from Yale and a respectable career as a biomedical scientist. He was solid, respectful and smart. A son-in-law any family would be proud of with skin the color of roasted chestnuts, and a smile as bright as Broadway lights. He was very charming and, on more than one occasion, Lewa wished he was hers. As a beverage scientist, she had a career she was proud of and a number of friends, but Stillman was one of the few individuals she felt easy with. But Lewa knew that her sister's marriage was solid and kept her fantasies to herself and briefly wished she didn't have to see the happily married pair this year. Besides, she didn't want another year of jollof rice, curried trout, plantain moi moi and pepper soup. She wanted a turkey like millions of other US families—even vegetarians celebrated with tofu that at least tasted like turkey.

Two weeks before Thanksgiving, Lewa listened with awe as her friend, Valerie, a fresh faced blonde from Wisconsin, described her upcoming feast while they sat in the cafeteria of their office building.

"Mashed potatoes, turkey, and cranberry sauce."

"What's the cranberry sauce for?" Lewa asked.

"It goes with the turkey."

Lewa didn't understand but nodded anyway. "Okay go on."

"Just the usual," Valerie shrugged, not understanding her friend's interest. "Cornbread, stuffing, ham, green beans."

Lewa sat back in her seat and sighed. "That sounds heavenly. I wish I could just be a fly on the wall."

"Would you like to come over?"

She sat up with interest. "Really?"

"Sure, we'll have plenty of food and I know my family won't mind."

"Perhaps you should ask your husband first."

Valerie laughed. "As long as he gets food, he doesn't care who shows up. I'm hosting his parents and trust me we'll have leftover for days." She grinned warming to the idea. "Yes, you should come. It will be fun."

Lewa sat back her hope slowly dwindling. "I'll think about it."

But she didn't have to think about it. Lewa knew she would have to ask her mother and she already had a good idea of how she would respond.

***

"No." Mrs. Olunlade said as she checked over the shopping list for the upcoming feast. They sat in the kitchen while their housegirl, Biti, carefully cleaned the special holiday dishes. Her mother was a small woman with delicate features that belied the mind of a sharp woman who had a successful nursing career and been married thirty-six years to a man who treated her well.

"But Mom. I've been invited."

Mrs. Olunlade did not look up from her list. She scribbled a note down. "And you can go another time. Thanksgiving is for family."

"But—"

She lifted her gaze and pointed her pen at Lewa. "And this time your grandmother will be able to join us. Would you want her to come all the way from Nigeria and not see you here?"

"She could see me on another day."

"She will see you on Thanksgiving." Mrs. Olunlade returned to her list, making it clear the discussion was finished.

Lewa sighed exasperated. Her mother could be as unmovable as a stone castle. "Then can we do something different   this   year?"

Mrs. Olunlade looked at her daughter suspicious. "Different?"

"Yes."

"Such as what?"

Lewa took a deep breath, then said in a rush. "Can we have a turkey?"

"For what?"

"To eat." Lewa tapped the table hoping to make her mother understand. "Mom, that's what people usually eat during Thanksgiving. A big delicious turkey. You've been here long enough to know that."

"But we always have curried trout and I thought you liked my seasonings."

"I do."

"And Aunty Elizabeth makes jollof rice."

"Yes."

"And Aunty Femi makes moi moi—"

"Mom, I know." Lewa sat forward and clasped her hands together, trying to show a piousness she didn't feel. "It's just that...just this once I'd like to have something different."

Mrs. Olunlade frowned. "I don't know how to cook a turkey."

"We could follow a recipe," Lewa said with a note of hope.

Mrs. Olunlade set her pen down and folded her arms. "Why are you worrying about food when you don't even have a husband to show your grandmother when she comes?"

Lewa fell back like a lead balloon. "You're changing the subject."

Mrs. Olunlade lifted her daughter's chin, her gaze softening. "You're so pretty and bright. What am I supposed to tell her?"

"You don't have to tell her anything."

"Mrs. Adeniyi has a son."

"No."

"You can't leave everything up to fate. The problem with you is that you haven't made it a priority and before you know it, it will be too late."

"I'm only thirty—"

Mrs. Olunlade quickly covered her daughter's mouth as if she'd said something foul. "Quiet. You don't look it and there's no reason to keep saying it. Do you think being over thirty and unmarried is a virtue?"

Lewa removed her mother's hand and kissed the back of her palm. "I'm sorry. I'll be more careful next time. Now, what about a turkey?"

Mrs. Olunlade's mouth quirked up in a quick grin, sensing her daughter's strategy to appease her. "I'll think it over. Go ask your father and see what he says."

***

"Dad, can we have a turkey for Thanksgiving this year?" She'd found him in the family room watching a NOVA special. She sat in the chair opposite him.

Mr. Olunlade was a large man with a soft spoken voice and his voice was even softer now. "What did your mother say?" he said with a note of caution.

"She told me to ask you."

He nodded then said, "How's work?"

"It's fine, now about the turkey—"

"Are you seeing anyone?"

Lewa blinked looking bored. "Dad."

"Does that mean no?"

Lewa shook her head. "No, I'm not seeing anyone, but I—"

"Why not? Why haven't you found someone to settle down with yet? You're a pretty woman and—" He pointed at her. "You must be doing something to scare them off. Do you tell them how much you make?"

Lewa affectionately squeeze her father's knee. "Dad, stop changing the subject. Can we have a turkey or not?"

He rubbed his chin, hesitant. "What did your mother say again?"

Lewa sighed, praying for patience. "She wanted to know your opinion."

A slow grin spread on his face. "That's rare. That means she's not sure. I say no. Let's stick with tradition."

"But that's my point. Jollof rice, moi moi and curried trout isn't traditional for Thanksgiving. Other people at least have a turkey."

"I don't care." He held up his hand like a feudal king making a decree. "It's the tradition for this house and it means a lot to our family. Do you know why we have jollof rice with curried trout?"

"No."

"Because trout was the first expensive meal I could afford. When I first came to this country I worked in a gas station. I hadn't met your mother yet and I stayed with Big Mummy's family. Finally I was able to get a promotion and the first thing I did was go to the local international store and purchase trout. So every Thanksgiving I buy that to remind me of how thankful I am."

***

"What did your father say?" Mrs. Olunlade said catching Lewa trying to sneak out of the house without saying goodbye.

"He told me a story about why we have jollof rice and trout."

"So his answer is no turkey?"

"Yes, he wants to keep our tradition."

Her mother beamed. "Good, but I've decided you're right. We should add something extra and I spoke to Femi and she's going to cook something you'll love."

"Really?" Lewa said clasping her hands together.

"Yes, she'll make samosas."

Lewa's hands fell to her sides. "But Mom that's Indian."

"Yes, exactly," her mother said pleased with her cleverness. "Didn't the English eat with the Indians?"

Lewa stood for a moment wondering if she should laugh or cry. "Yes...no...not East Indians. They ate with American Indians. Native Americans."

But her mother had stopped listening. She adjusted the collar of Lewa's coat. "She's excited because she knows it's one of your favorites. See, I do listen and can be flexible."

Lewa sighed. "Thanks Mom."

Mrs. Olunlade called the housegirl, Biti, and handed her the list. "I want only the best."

She bowed appropriately submissive. "Yes, ma'am." Although only nineteen, she looked ten years older and had stooped shoulders.

Lewa kissed her mother on the cheek then left.

Once she and Biti were both outside, Lewa gently slapped the younger woman in the back. "How many times do I have to tell you to stand up straight?"

"Sorry Aunty." She rubbed her hands together, and wrapped her scarf tighter. "I still have to get used to the cold."

Lewa glanced up at the red and yellow leaves clinging to the trees, feeling the crisp November air against her skin. "You weren't cold in the house, so stop lying."

"Sorry Aunty."

"Always stand tall." Lewa walked to her car.

"Aunty?"

She turned. "Yes?"

"Why do you want a turkey?" Biti asked making a face. "Isn't that just bland English food?"

Lewa laughed at the girl's expression, knowing she wouldn't understand. "Goodbye, Biti," she said then jumped in her car.

***

"Just forget about the damn turkey and eat what you're given," Lewa's friend Hannah Lee said as she, Lewa and Valerie changed in the gym locker after swimming. She'd known Hannah since they met at the university and could always depend on her for straight talk. "The holidays aren't meant to be enjoyed. If you're having fun, you're not doing it right. It's about family, fights and feasting. You just grin and bear it."

"I don't mind spending time with my family, and I don't mind them bothering me about a husband," Lewa said. "I've gotten used to it."

"You're braver than I am," Hannah said. "If I hadn't met my boyfriend in time I would have made him up."

"Yes, being single on the holidays is the worse," Valerie said.

Lewa rolled her eyes. "Thanks for your support."

"No, I don't mean you. I mean in general. It makes you an easy target."

"I can take being a target, if I could just get something different to eat. Is having a turkey so wrong?"

"It's not what they're used to," Hannah said. "We don't have mashed potatoes we have sticky rice."

Lewa rested her chin in her hand. "At least you have a turkey."

***

So it was clear. Thanksgiving meant many different things to different people. To Hannah it was sticky rice and family fights. To Valerie, a warm family gathering and traditional American food. To her father, jollof rice and trout reminded him of all he was grateful for. Thanksgiving was a symbolic day of family and blessings. Her parents had no connection to the story of turkey and mashed potatoes, and maybe she was grasping at a story that wasn't hers either. She needed her own special dish.

A week before Thanksgiving she bought a turkey.

"So what are you going to do with it?" her younger sister Arielle asked while the two woman stared at the frozen bird on Lewa's kitchen counter. "It's huge."

"I know." Lewa poked it. "And I'm not sure what I'm going to do yet."

"Why do you want a turkey so bad anyway? You can have turkey any other day."

"It's not the same."

"And why are you making it so complicated? If you wanted turkey why not just buy a cooked one?"

"Because I want to do it myself."

"You could get burned."

Lewa looked at her sister curious. "How could I get burned?"

"It happens every year. People get burned trying to cook their turkeys."

"That's only if they're deep frying them," Lewa said playfully hitting her. "Stop being so negative. If you don't want to help, why did you come over?"

"I'm curious."

Lewa lifted the turkey and put it back in the freezer. "I'm curious about something too." She closed the freezer door and looked at her sister. "Are you ever going to tell Mom and Dad about the miscarriage?"

Arielle sat down at the kitchen table and tugged on one of her braids with nervous fingers. "Why would I?"

"Then they won't bother you about starting a family." Lewa sat in front of her. "I know it must get on your nerves."

"I don't want them to blame me," she said in a choked voice.

"Why would they blame you?" Lewa said surprised by her sister's worry. "At least they'll know you're trying and they may be more sensitive."

"The Aunts won't be."

Lewa sighed recognizing the truth of her sister's words. The Aunts would be harder to convince. "You will have your own family soon."

"Aunty Elizabeth will blame me for not eating the right foods, Mom will say it's because I'm too old and should have started sooner." Tears filled her eyes.

Lewa covered her sister's hand. "But we know that none of that is true," she said in a soft voice. "You haven't done anything wrong. And you and Stillman will be fine."

Arielle brushed away her tears and lowered her eyes. "It's caused a strain between us."

"Of course," Lewa said giving her sister's hand a reassuring squeeze. "It's a stressful time for many couples."

"No, I mean...he's not handling it well. He's getting pressure from his family too and I'm afraid he'll start blaming me as well."

Lewa stiffened and sat back. "He's supposed to be your support not your judge. Do you want me to talk to him?"

Arielle lifted her gaze, suddenly wary. "What would you say?"

"Treat my little sister right or I'll punch you in the face."

Arielle smiled then laughed. "You're so silly."

Lewa returned her smile glad she could lighten the mood. "You're good together. You're a great couple. I don't want this to pull you apart."

"You can't stop it, if it does."

"It won't. "

"But what if I can never carry a baby? Sheba is already on her third," she said referring to a cousin of theirs.

Lewa brushed the idea aside with a quick flick of her wrist. "It's too soon to think like that."

Arielle shook her head. "No, it's not. I asked him and he said that if I couldn't have a child then we wouldn't have a marriage."

"He didn't mean that."

"He did."

"What about adoption or surrogacy?"

"He doesn't want to adopt and we can't afford surrogacy. Unless..."

"Unless what?"

"We could find someone to help us," she said looking at her sister with a hopeful expression.

Lewa shook her head, resisting the urge to jump up and run out of the room. "No way. Don't look at me. I'm not ready for that."

"This may be your only chance," Arielle said suddenly eager. "You're older than me and we both know your prospects are slim."

"Thank you Mom," Lewa said in a sour tone.

"I just want you to consider it. If you could do this we'd both appreciate it."

***

Lewa let her sister's words hang in her mind. Having a baby was something Arielle really wanted and if it could help her marriage it would be worth it, right? But then part of Lewa was angry that her sister had to find another alternative. Couldn't Stillman be more patient? Couldn't they come up with something together? Would he really leave Arielle if she couldn't bare his children? Would a child really change all that? Did he love her sister or was she just an appendage to him? A status symbol?

Lewa had to find out for herself so she met her brother-in-law at his office and treated him to lunch.

Once they'd placed their orders she said, "Do you love my sister?"

Stillman looked at her surprised and baffled. "You know I do."

"Then why are you threatening to leave her?"

He paused then said, "I didn't say that."

"Then what did you say? I know about the problem between you two."

He glanced around as if afraid someone might overhear them. "Do we have to discuss this here?"

"No, we can go to your place and I can talk to you with Arielle there. Or I can wait until Thanksgiving and let the whole family give their opinions."

Stillman held up his hands in surrender. "All I said was that having my own children means a lot to me." He let his hands fall. "It's something I've always wanted and it's expected."

"Dreams can change."

"Not this one. Being a father to my own flesh and blood is what I want."

"She really wants to have children with you. But can you love her enough if she can't?"

"We are thinking about surrogacy."

"Yes, she told me. And that hasn't answered my question."

"I don't mind doing that," he said expertly avoiding a question he didn't want to answer. "If she can't do it herself." His gaze trailed the length of Lewa.

Lewa took a sip of her drink. "Take the thought out of your mind and bury it."

He shrugged. "It's been done before and it would really help us a lot."

"I'm older than her."

"But you're better built to carry children," he said making a curving motion with his hands.

Lewa held up her hand and pointed at him, unable to stop a smile. "Watch it."

He grinned. "It's a compliment. If I hadn't met your sister first, maybe—"

Lewa laughed. "I used to think that too, but now I know it wouldn't have worked."

He frowned. "What do you mean?"

She shook her head, knowing she wouldn't be able to explain it to him. She was only starting to understand it herself. "I'll see what I can do."

"Arielle told me you bought a turkey for Thanksgiving."

"I'm not sure what I'll do with it yet."

"You'll come up with something." He winked. "You always do."

***

That evening, Lewa sat in her kitchen and pondered her conversations with Stillman and Arielle. And as she thought, she discovered a truth about herself too. That she didn't really want her sister's husband, just the status he brought her. She didn't want to get married—at least not yet. She was enjoying her life and truly never thought about being a wife and mother the way other women did. Her former desire for a husband had been a way for her to fit in. A way to stop being so different. It was the same with the turkey. She wanted their home to have the same sights and smells as other homes, but for what purpose? Was it wrong to be different?

Lewa loved Stillman. He was a wonderful, generous man, but she now realized he was more traditional than she'd thought—than she'd allowed herself to see. His values matched her sister's perfectly. Despite their easy conversation and ambitions, he would be a terrible match for her. She could only hope that the right man was out there. If not...her family would continue to feel sorry for her. She'd be a failure, a half person, but she didn't mind anymore because she had a private joy no one could take from her. A joy of being authentically herself. She didn't want her sister's private fears that she wasn't a complete woman if she couldn't bear children or Stillman's fears of how he'd be perceived. Even if they did have a child, Lewa knew it wouldn't be enough. They'd be expected to have at least two. To live others expectations could be exhausting and Lewa was ready to remove herself from that race.

Lewa called her sister. "Try for another year. If you're still having trouble, I'll pay for a surrogate."

"Thank you," Arielle said with tears in her voice.

"Just be prepared for the Aunts this year."

"I am. What are you going to do about the turkey? I think you should donate it."

"I could, but I'm not going to. We're having turkey this year one way or another. I'll see you Thursday." Lewa hung up then opened her freezer and stared at her frozen turkey with renewed determination. Authenticity, that would be her contribution to this year's holiday dinner.

***

Lewa went online and looked at different recipes and spent many hours looking at cooking clips. But she still didn't find anything that would suit her family. She decided to go to the store and stood in the baking section staring at the deep fryers, beakers and thermometers. She knew cooking was a science, but she felt like a novice in the lab of a genius. Even if she got the turkey right she didn't know anything about stuffing or glazing. She wanted to create something her family would eat, something familiar yet a little different. Unfortunately, she didn't know what.

"Can I help you?" a sales associate said. He looked like a college student and had shaggy red hair he kept having to push back from his eyes.

"No, I'm just looking."

"Okay," he said then started to turn.

"Wait," Lewa said before he left. "What do you do for Thanksgiving?"

He shrugged. "Watch football and eat turkey."

"Right," Lewa said. *Just like millions.*

"But that's not my favorite part," he said with a shy grin as if hesitant to share.

"What is?" she urged him.

"It's the leftovers. My mom always buys two huge tur-keys 'cause we have a lot of guests, but we still end up with a lot of leftover turkey. The real fun is all the things she does with it."

Lewa stepped closer intrigued. "Like what?"

He brushed his hair back and thought for a moment. "Turkey sandwiches, turkey pie, turkey enchiladas. You can do a lot."

He was right. She could do a lot. She was thinking of the turkey as something whole that couldn't be altered, but who said she had to bake it like everyone else? She could treat it like the basis of 'anything,' making her options limitless. "Thank you," she said grabbing a big baking pan then pushing her cart into the main aisle. "Have a great Thanksgiving."

"You too."

Before going home, Lewa stopped at the international market and grabbed a packet of melon seeds and chili pepper then went home and baked the turkey—following a recipe she'd found—while she chopped a bowl full of miniature tomatoes and onions. She couldn't wait to show her family her new tradition.

***

That Thanksgiving, Lewa boldly set her turkey dish on the table among the red jollof rice and yellow curried trout.

"What is this?" her mother asked as Lewa took the foil off.

Lewa looked at her mother with love, seeing the unease in her eyes. It would be another year before her sister gave birth to a boy and three years after that before Lewa walked down the aisle to an American man her family accepted with some hesitation, but none of those things—her sister's childless state or her unmarried one—mattered to her that day. She finally knew who she was and what Thanksgiving meant to her. She was thankful for the freedom to be a her own person—to be unique and different without shame. Now she had her own special dish that would add to the season of traditions.

"It's meat pies," Aunty Elizabeth said recognizing a familiar staple.

"It's turkey pies," Lewa corrected. "Spiced with chili peppers and I added some other ingredients."

"They look good," her father said.

"I bet they'll be delicious," Stillman added.

"You'll make a good wife," her grandmother said.

But this time Lewa didn't mind the mention of her single state. She looked at her sister and Stillman, with no envy. The man for her was out there, somewhere. And if he wasn't, she was okay with that too. She'd gotten her turkey for Thanksgiving and hopefully started a new tradition. One that suited her just fine.

The Other Woman

The size 42DDD wasn't hers.

Andrea Hartnett looked at the bright pink bra she'd found in her top lingerie drawer wondering if she should feel perplexed or enraged. If her husband was cheating, why would this bra end up in *her* drawer? Wasn't it something a wife would find underneath the bed, in the backseat of a car, or in her husband's jacket pocket?

If there was another explanation, what could it be? They'd had two kids—ages five and seven—within ten years of marriage and the thrill was definitely gone. Andrea glanced out the bedroom window as the descending darkness of night slowly devoured a bleak winter sun. Boredom settled on them some days more than others, but was that anyone's fault? Wasn't that normal? Robert was a good man, good husband and father.

But had he gotten tired of it all?

Had he met someone at the play dates he went to with the kids?

Was this his way of rebelling against his role as a house-husband? The arrangement worked for them, but at times she wondered if he missed an outside work life. If he missed being an electrical engineer and the chance to discuss the newest changes in his field, instead of the latest action figure. She knew he'd finished his holiday shopping—he was always orderly and regimented—she hadn't even started hers.

Should she confront him or be subtle? Andrea turned the object over in her hand, seeing the lacy white trim, feeling the satin finish, a flash of something crossing her thoughts—a familiar sensation or memory—before it was quickly gone. How could one be subtle about something like this? Did she approach him in the kitchen and calmly say, "Darling, I found someone else's bra in my drawer? Do you know how that happened?"

Did she really want to know?

Did she just want to pretend?

Andrea hurriedly shoved the bra back in the drawer when she heard footsteps approaching. Moments later, Robert, came into the room carrying a laundry basket stacked with freshly washed clothes that reminded her of the scent of tulips and roses in the sunshine. He set the basket on the bed then lifted up her cream blouse and held it up with a flourish. "Tada!" he said with a big grin, his teeth white against his cocoa skin.

She frowned. "What?"

"I got the wine stain out."

Yes, she remembered being upset that she'd ruined the blouse after only one wear. She'd been at a holiday office party where her colleague, Mona Shan, had gotten tipsy and splashed Andrea's blouse. Mona had apologized profusely, but Andrea silently wondered if she was really apologizing for getting the promotion Andrea had worked two years for. But Andrea had laughed and made a joke, pretending that nothing bothered her and the tense moment was quickly forgotten.

But she hadn't forgotten it. The wine stain and Mona's sloppy apology burned in her chest like acid. That evening, Robert had found her sitting on the side of their bed in tears. She told him about the stain, not the lost promotion, not the catty remarks her boss sometimes made about her performance or even how tired she felt sometimes, and he'd squeezed her shoulder and said, "Don't worry, I can get the stain out."

And now he had and she wondered if it mattered. She stared at the clean, crisp blouse amazed that he'd managed to make it look as if it were brand new. Was size 42DDD someone who knew the best way to get stains out? Did she know the healthiest 'green' cleaning solution for counter-tops? Was she younger? Did she make him feel more like a man?

"Thanks," she said, plastering on a smile.

But the smile didn't fool him. "What's wrong?"

"Why?"

"You look tired."

I'm not tired, she wanted to say. I'm sad. Sad that we're keeping secrets. She went to the drawer to pull out the bra then stopped. She couldn't confront him now. She didn't want to be angry. She knew talks never worked when emotion came first. "I just had a long day."

"Dinner's almost ready."

The scent of curried rice and the sweetness of mango chutney floated up the stairs. "Smells great."

He winked. "Tastes good too," he said then turned.

Andrea watched him leave wondering if 42DDD had also tried his cooking.

***

She thought about leaving the bra on his pillow. Since she left for work after dropping the kids off at school it wouldn't be hard to do. But he might not see it or—worse—make anything of it. She thought of leaving it between the couch cushions where he watched TV, but then the kids might find it. She thought about taking a picture and sending it to his cell phone with a message: Who does this belong to?

She thought of checking his phone for private texts. She thought of calling in sick and following him around all day.

But she didn't do any of those things. Instead, she pretended like nothing had changed. On the weekend she watched him—building a snowman in the front yard, hanging holiday lights along the house trim, wiping Kendall's tears when he slipped on the ice and hit his head, and vacuuming the car. He was a man in constant motion while she felt as if she were standing still. At times they passed each other like strangers.

And she let two more days pass without mentioning the pink bra, wondering when she'd smell the whiff of someone else's perfume on his shirt (would it be spicy, musky or sweet?), see a lipstick stain on his collar (bright pink, deep red or purple?), but he'd be too smart for that. He did the laundry and knew how to take stains out. She wondered when she would catch him quickly hanging up the phone when she entered the room. When would she catch him in a lie?

They'd never lied to each before. Even when they'd first met as interns at her first job out of college, they'd been honest with each other about their ambitions and hopes for the future. She remembered when she'd gotten the dream job she'd applied for and how proud he'd been to support her and her career. All things seemed possible back then.

Had she made him feel devalued? She remembered the time he'd gone on a weekend fishing trip with his brother and she realized how much she depended on him. She didn't know what to do with the kids or what to feed them. She had breakfast, lunch and dinner delivered the entire weekend. When she told him about her harrowing time, he'd just laughed and the next time he was gone for the weekend, he prepared the meals in advance and left instructions.

But had that bothered him? Did he think she was useless? Was 42DDD a domestic goddess? Did she have children? Was she married too? Divorced? She'd seen some of the other mothers and the teachers at their children's school. None looked like a 42DDD, but there were plenty who were fresh faced and pretty and young.

The questions continued to loom and grow until she couldn't ignore them anymore.

***

She confronted him one evening after he'd put the kids to bed and was relaxing on the couch watching a science special about galaxies. In the background, the Christmas tree glowed with colored lights, its branches heavy under the weight of ornaments both store bought and handmade. The scent of peppermint from the candy canes their kids had devoured earlier still lingered in the air.

"I found this in my drawer," she said, holding out the bra.

He looked at her—not the bra—for a long minute then said, "I wondered when you'd say something."

"Who…wait what?"

"I didn't think you cared."

"You put this there?"

He nodded.

"Why?"

He shrugged. "Just wanted to see what you'd do."

She waved the bra in his face, fighting back tears of hurt and anger. "Is this how you wanted to tell me you're having an affair?"

His brows shot up. "An affair?"

"Yes, with this woman."

He sat up, confused. "What woman?"

She flung the bra at him. "The woman who wears this!"

He caught it and briefly hung his head, rubbing his forehead. "There's no..." He let his hand fall to his lap then looked up at her. "I love the woman who owns this, but she doesn't wear it anymore."

He loved this other woman? What did he mean she didn't wear it anymore? Had she left him? And why had he put it in her drawer? Again a flash of something—an emotion or memory she wasn't sure—coursed through her thoughts before disappearing. "I don't understand."

He took a deep breath. "So you don't recognize it?"

"Why would I recognize someone else's bra?"

"Because it's not someone else's. It's yours. Was yours." He paused. "From before."

She froze, a slow dawning casting aside the cobwebs of her mind and the flashing thoughts began to connect and take shape. She didn't need to ask 'Before what?' because she knew: Before she had her breast reduction surgery. Before she was left with scars that made her feel ugly. Before she realized that the surgery had relieved her back pain, but not the other pains in her life.

She felt tears build, tightening her throat, wetting her eyes, as she realized she had been the one with secrets, not him. They'd agreed to keep the bra as a reminder of all they'd come through together. To remind her of the past she'd left behind. She'd bought the bra years ago as a new bride and had never worn it—or had she worn it once?—before tucking it away. She'd forgotten it. The woman who'd bought it felt like a stranger to her.

"You know I love you no matter what," he said. "I supported your decision."

"I know." But she'd pushed him away anyway. She'd let words of warning from others shove aside his words of comfort.

"Don't do it," she remembered one woman say in a support group. "My husband left me after I did it. Men have a harder time with the change than we do."

"It was the best decision I made," another countered.

"But you're single," the first woman argued.

"Men started looking at me different and I'm still getting used to it," a third said. She'd later developed a drinking problem and was now in therapy for that.

And the closer Andrea got to the date of her surgery, the more unsolicited comments she heard, or had they just gotten louder? She wasn't sure; she just remembered that each syllable felt like darts.

"I don't know why she'd get rid of what lots of women pay to have," she overheard a family friend say.

"I'm not surprised she's the one wearing the pants in that house now. She cut off her breasts and he cut off his balls," she'd overheard a great-aunt say at a family dinner.

"I'd never let my wife do it," a second cousin said.

But she went through with her decision gaining strength from her husband's support. Not knowing that his support wouldn't be enough. That a new pain would replace the old one.

She'd changed her entire wardrobe to accommodate the new woman she'd become, but inside she still felt as invisible as she once had been. In the past, she had to deal with people who didn't think women with big breasts had a brain. She'd had to endure snickers all through high school and college from both teachers and students. She'd had to tolerate guys who'd ask her out expecting only one thing and shouted angry slurs at her when they didn't get it.

Robert had been different. He'd called her beautiful. He looked at her face and not just her chest. He thought she was smart. But she no longer felt beautiful and now she didn't feel smart. She wondered if he'd noticed that too? She sat down beside him no longer able to hold his gaze. "I didn't get the promotion," she said in a soft voice.

He blinked. "What?"

She bit her lip then looked at him. "The night I got the wine stain on my blouse, that's when I found out."

Anger lit his brown eyes. "But you'd worked your ass off for that new client and you've brought in millions of dollars to that company."

"I know," she said, glad he sounded as outraged as she'd felt. "It wasn't enough."

"If they won't value you, then you need to start looking for another position that will."

"What if it pays less?"

"And I can't stay home?" he said, finishing her real question.

She nodded, holding her breath.

"What if it pays more?"

She hadn't thought of that, but she held her breath because he still hadn't given her an answer.

He covered her hand with his. "All that matters to me is your happiness and our family, you know that."

She'd let herself forget. She glanced at the 42DDD she'd placed beside her, remembering the woman she used to be. The woman he'd fallen in love with and who had fallen in love with him. For all her pain, that woman had laughed more and lived more.

Andrea turned to her husband and hugged him, inhaling his scent. He used to smell like aftershave and leather; now he smelled like crayons and fresh coffee. She felt the strength of his embrace when his arms encircled her waist and she wondered how long it had been since she'd let him hold her this close. She closed her eyes.

There hadn't been another woman. Or rather she had to face the other woman she used to be and not fear or hate her…

"Thank you," she said, but what she really meant was 'I love you'.

Fortunately, Robert knew that and said 'I love you too' without words, pressing his lips against hers, letting his body say what words couldn't.

And the other woman faded away, in the hushed, warm silence of the evening, as they renewed their vows and discovered each other in an exciting new way. Andrea realized she still had many questions. She still had to get her holiday shopping done and they had a lot of decisions to make for the future. But one thing she did know for certain, which suddenly made everything seem bright and beautiful, was that she didn't have to fear losing him…or herself…again.

The Perfect Christmas

He didn't like the sight of the stones. Although they looked innocent as they lay on the front doorstep, glittering under the cold rays of a winter sun, they reminded him of something, but he couldn't remember what, that left him with a feeling of dread.

"What are those?"

Kenneth Preston turned to his wife, Jessie, as she came up behind him carrying two bags in each hand, her red winter hat tipped at an angle. They'd been holiday shopping for their adopted daughter, Syrah. It was to be their first Christmas together as a family and they were both eager to make it special. He didn't want anything to ruin it. Somehow he felt the stones would do that.

"Probably nothing," he said, bending down to remove the stones.

She grabbed his arm. "Wait. Don't touch them."

"Jasmine, don't—" he said calling her by her given name. Only he was allowed to call her that.

She stepped closer, putting her two bags in one hand, and gazed down at the stones. "Just give me a minute."

He didn't want to. He didn't like the look of interest in her gaze. The stones were bad news, he could feel it.

Kenneth put the keys in the lock and opened the front door. "Come on, it's cold."

"I wonder who left them here. The arrangement is very peculiar." She bent closer to examine them.

His wife had a special gift and affinity with stones. He respected that, but not now. He wanted her for Syrah and himself. He didn't want to share her attention with anyone. Especially someone who'd left a strange puzzle on their doorstep. A puzzle that reminded him of something, but he didn't know what. "Jasmine, we need to put the bags away before Ace gets home," he said, using Syrah's nickname.

She scooped up the stones in her gloved hand and offered him a bright smile. "Coming, coming." She brushed past him into the welcoming warmth of their house, the scent of sugar and ginger greeting them. But as he closed the door behind her, he felt as if the cold chill of winter had followed them inside.

***

"What are you going to do with the stones?" Kenneth asked Jessie later that evening as they prepared for bed. He didn't really want to know, but couldn't help his curiosity.

She slipped under the bed sheets and rested against the headboard. "Nothing. I don't know who they're from or why they were left."

He swallowed, hoping she was telling him the truth. Was it a warning? Had the scandal about his past created still more consequences for them to face? He felt a fissure of unease, like a tiny, hair-thin crack in a piece of glass. A crack of a memory wanting to emerge from the corner of his mind where he'd safely kept his past sealed. But he fought it; he wanted to stay in the present. They'd come through so much. He didn't want anything to separate them again. "Are you sure?"

"Am I sure of what?"

"That you don't know anything?"

Jessie held his gaze, a quick flash of fire lighting them. "You think I'm lying?"

Kenneth lowered his gaze and swallowed. He didn't want to argue. He didn't want to upset her because he was afraid. Afraid of… He inwardly groaned. He didn't know what. But something ugly gripped him, something frightening and troubling. He didn't want anything to destroy the perfect Christmas he planned for them. Nothing could go wrong. He wouldn't let it. The memory teetering on the edge of his mind would stay there. He smiled, bent forward and kissed her. "No, I wouldn't dare. I—I just don't like the look of them."

"They're nothing to worry about."

He nodded and slipped in beside her, taking deep breaths. He had to believe her. Although he didn't like the stones, he had to trust her. He couldn't think she knew something and wasn't telling him. He couldn't think that maybe she was protecting him. He had to believe that there weren't secrets between them. That was the past. They were now joined together for life. He'd need two thousand lifetimes to show her how much he loved her. This Christmas would be the start of many—nothing could go wrong. Unless…

"What's the matter?" Jessie said in sharp tone.

"What?"

"You stopped breathing."

Kenneth froze. "I did?"

"Yes. Why? You always do that when you're upset."

He avoided her gaze. "I was just thinking about something."

"What?"

He shook his head. "Nothing." He gripped his hand into a fist. He was already lying to her and he didn't want to, but felt that he must. Trust meant not asking questions, and he couldn't doubt her.

"I won't do anything without telling you first," she said as if reading his mind.

He took a deep breath. "I know." He kissed her again, assuring her as much as himself. "Promise me anyway," he whispered against her lips.

She smiled. "Promise."

He felt some of his tension ease, then turned off the lamp light, but the darkness that settled around them seemed to find its way inside him too.

***

And that darkness still followed him a week later. He didn't know why the stones bothered him or why he felt suddenly restless. He stared at his reflection in the full-length closet mirror, straightening his tie one morning as he prepared for work, almost not recognizing the man staring back at him. Only a couple of weeks earlier he'd been so happy about the upcoming holiday and now he was filled with dread.

He left the large closet and walked into the bedroom, then felt someone grab his arm and pin it behind him. "Tell me what's bothering you," a female voice whispered in his ear.

Kenneth couldn't help a smile as his pulse quickened; he could overpower his wife in one swift move, but he'd let her believe she was in control, for now. "Should something be bothering me?"

She tightened her hold. "You tell me. You haven't been yourself the last few days."

"Nothing's wrong."

"Want to arm wrestle?"

He slipped out of her grasp, swung her over his shoulder and pinned her to the ground. He gazed down at her with a smug grin. "Want to lose?"

He waited to see her temper flare. Watched to see her beautiful brown gaze turn hot. She'd probably make him late for work and he'd enjoy every minute of it. But instead of her typical heated look, he saw worry tinge her eyes.

"I feel you pulling away from me," she said.

He didn't move, the truth of her words holding him still. She was right. He could feel it himself and didn't know why. They were now married, she was his new wife and he loved their life together and yet something gnawed at him and seemed to grow the closer Christmas came. His fears seemed foolish and there was still so much yet to know about each other, but there were still things he didn't want her to know.

Because he had no words, he kissed her, lingering over the sweet taste of her mouth, hoping it would be enough to remove the worry from her eyes. He wanted her to think about the tall pine they'd decorated that stood in their living room, the colored lights that covered the house, and the apple cider they'd had by the fire. The holidays were supposed to be happy, especially this one. He'd keep whatever darkness that hovered, within him. He drew away from her and smiled. "How can I be pulling away, when I'm right here?"

Her gaze searched his, the worry deepened. "Kenneth, what's wrong?"

His pulse quickened again, this time from fear instead of desire. *Why did she have to know him so well?* "I can't stop thinking about the stones," he said, releasing her.

Jessie sat up. "I think I may know who the stones belong to. One of the clients at the store may have left them because he heard about me and—"

"I don't want you to have anything to do with him." He didn't mean to sound harsh, but something told him it was important that she stay away.

He waited for her to argue. Waited for her to tell him that he was her husband and not her jailor and that she'd do what she wanted to do.

Instead, she nodded. "Okay."

"What?"

"I said okay. If it bothers you that much, I'll leave them, but..."

"But what?"

"I sense that whoever left the stones seems to want protection and help. They're not dangerous and—"

Kenneth shook his head. "I don't care. Stay away."

"Fine. I will." Jessie lightly touched his cheek, her fingers warm and soft against his skin. "Is that all that's bothering you?"

God, he hoped so. He took a deep breath and stood. "I'd better get going." He lifted her to her feet, resisting the urge to hold her close in case he wouldn't let her go.

***

There was too much snow. It wouldn't stop. It was two days to Christmas and it seemed people would get the white Christmas they hoped for. But to Kenneth, the continuous snowfall chilled him. It didn't fall with a soft light touch, but seemed to pound the earth, suffocating everything around him in white.

"Dad, are you okay?"

The sound of his daughter's voice caused him both pleasure and pain, reminding him of what they'd both gained and lost. But he couldn't think about his brother, Eddie, right now. Nothing else mattered except making Syrah happy and helping her forget her brutal past. He turned from the window and looked at her as she stood there, wearing an oversized sweater he'd wanted to donate but she'd decided to keep. Their dog, Dion, stood by her side. Kenneth forced a smile. "Of course I am."

She bit her lip. "I'm not."

He forced his smile not to waver. "Why not?"

She sent a nervous glance towards the window. "They were supposed to work, but I'm not sure they will."

"What are you talking about?"

She shook her head. "Nothing."

"What's wrong?"

She looked at him. "Mom's not home yet."

He checked his watch. He'd assumed she was upstairs. Jessie was usually home before him. "I'm sure she'll be here soon."

He couldn't let Syrah sense his unease. He knew she was looking forward to their first Christmas as a family, and was used to being disappointed. Did she have the same fear he did? That happiness may be out of reach for them? They both loved Jessie, but they also both knew that the ones they loved could hurt them the most. He knelt in front of

Syrah, keeping his smile in place and his tone light as he pressed down his own concerns. "I bet she had to finish up her holiday shopping and lost track of time."

Syrah nodded. "Yes, it's going to be all right, right?"

He tweaked her chin. "Right."

But an hour later, Kenneth wasn't so sure.

"I'm sure it's nothing," Jessie's eldest sister, Michelle, said when he called her. Her tone was practical and no-nonsense, reflecting the businesswoman she was. "She's a walking accident. If you worry about her, you'll grow old fast—trust me. Just wait for her to come home. If anything's happened, you'll know."

When he called Jessie's other sister, Teresa, the advice was the same but said in a lighter more soothing way. She was a woman who believed in visions and herbs and that reflected in her words. "Your years together have only just begun, your paths are intertwined and you're bound together unless you break them."

He gripped the phone. That didn't make any sense. "Just let me know if you hear from her."

"I will, but you have to trust her."

"Of course I trust her."

"With everything?"

He briefly shut his eyes. Teresa was sweet, but strange and he hadn't called for marriage advice. "Yes."

"Good, then she'll be fine. You both will."

But when another hour passed, he didn't feel fine. And his worry grew. He called her cousins and then anyone else he could think of, but no one could reach her. He had to believe that nothing was wrong. That she hadn't defied him and seen the man she'd mentioned about the stones against his wishes.

He had to believe that she was okay, even when another hour passed and he saw a story on the news about a woman's body being found near the bay.

"Poor woman," Freda, his housekeeper said, passing by the family room to head to the kitchen.

It couldn't be Jessie. She was just somewhere where her phone didn't work and the snow…

Kenneth looked out the window, his hard gaze sweeping over the snow blanketing the ground and weighing the trees with its oppressive white hand. It looked harmless, but it could be so many things. Why did he hate snow so much? He felt an answer to that question as the hair-thin crack of memory tried to expand in his mind, but he violently silenced it with his will.

In two days they'd have their first Christmas as a family. A Christmas to help him forget the pain of his past. He had the right to be happy, to fight for his joy and his place in the world.

As a child, he remembered one winter clearing the driveway for Jessie's family, the Cliftons. Eddie had promised to do it—and taken the advanced payment Mr. Clifton had given him—but did only half the job. Kenneth had finished it up, hoping nobody would notice. He made sure there was not a flake left.

"You mustn't try so hard," Mr. Clifton had told him with a glint in his eye.

He didn't understand him at first and felt a little hurt and defensive. He was embarrassed that he'd gotten caught and angered by the criticism.

"You'll wear yourself out for no reason." He now knew what Jessie's father had meant. That he didn't have to try so hard to please, to be accepted, but it was still a lesson he was learning. He wanted this Christmas to be one of the best Jessie and Syrah had ever had.

Three hours later, he paced. He couldn't report Jessie missing. Not yet. Not ever, he corrected. Because she would be home soon. She had to be.

Another hour passed. He felt himself falling apart. He grabbed his keys, determined to find her, then stopped when he heard the front door open.

He met her at the door. "Where have you been? We've been waiting for hours. Do you know how worried Ace was?" he said. "I had to lie to her to get her to eat dinner then lie to her again to get her to go to sleep. Do you know how many people I called? You couldn't let anyone know where you've been, what you were up to? What happened?"

Jessie blinked, then sighed with regret. "I hardly understood a word you said. But I know you're upset and I'm sorry. Now take a deep breath and speak slowly and in English."

It took Kenneth a moment to realize he'd spoken in French. The language of his youth, the language of his heart. He could feel himself shaking as his anger and fear mingled within his veins. He hadn't shouted at her like that before and always tried to be careful to control his temper. He knew the danger of losing control. He took her advice and took a deep breath. As he exhaled, he felt his shield of anger slip away, as if a filter had been removed from his eyes, and he finally saw his wife clearly.

He saw the cut on her lip and the bruise on her cheek and his heart twisted. He rushed towards her, then stopped himself from touching her. "What happened?"

Jessie pressed her hands together as if in prayer. "Don't be angry."

Kenneth folded his arms. "I'm already angry, what did you do?"

"This older woman was getting mugged—"

His arms fell to his sides. "You went after a mugger?"

"She said her life was in that purse and I couldn't just stand around and do nothing." Jessie held up her hand before he spoke. "I know he could have had a knife or a gun, but he didn't. Unfortunately, he got away and she was so shaken that she asked me to go with her to the police and I did. I'm sorry, I didn't even think to call you. And then on my way home, a car swerved and hit me. Not too bad, so don't worry, and then my phone died and it was just chaos. But I left the hospital because I wanted to come home."

His voice cracked in surprise. "You were at the hospital?"

"The woman who hit me was insistent I get checked by a doctor, so I just did it to calm her. I'm so sorry I didn't get in touch with you somehow. It was just a crazy day and—"

Kenneth spun away and headed upstairs.

Jessie followed him. "You're not going to forgive me?"

He headed for their bedroom. "I'm glad you're home."

"But you're still angry," she said, staying close behind.

He kept walking.

"Kenneth."

"Keep your voice down."

"Why? Syrah's probably already awake after your shouting rampage. At least she knows I'm home."

"It wasn't a rampage."

"It came close and I don't know why—"

"A woman was found dead today," he cut in, his voice raw with emotion, "and I thought it was you."

"Why would you think that?"

"I don't know!" And he truly didn't. He didn't understand his lingering anger. She was safe, but his heart still hammered in his ears.

"Why are you shouting at me again?"

"I'm not shouting."

"It's my fault!" another voice said. They both turned and saw Syrah standing at the end of the hallway. Her voice broke. "It's all my fault."

Jessie shook her head and walked towards her. "Honey, no it's not. We're just—"

She took a step back before Jessie could reach her. "I had Freda leave the stones on the doorstep, but they didn't work."

"What are you talking about?" Jessie asked.

"I know I don't have your gift with stones, but when Aunt Teresa told me that they were special stones that could bring good luck and protection to a house, I thought…" Her words fell away. "I was wrong."

"That's why they had that feeling," Jessie mumbled to herself. "I'd wondered about that." She knelt in front of Syrah. "You weren't wrong. And you didn't do anything bad. But why would you think we'd need that? What are you frightened of?"

Kenneth came up behind Jessie and cupped Syrah's chin before she could reply. "You're safe now."

Jessie hugged her. "You don't need to be afraid. We're a family now and we're happy." Jessie turned and looked up at Kenneth. "Right?"

He looked at Jessie then shifted his gaze to Syrah, a chill coursing through him. He knew what he had to say, even though he didn't mean it. "Yes." He kissed her on the forehead. "Now go back to bed or I'll take one of your presents away."

Syrah wrapped her arms around Jessie's neck and hugged her. "I'm so glad you're home."

Jessie hugged her back. "Me too."

***

"Kenneth, I said I'm sorry," Jessie said, closing the door behind them once they were alone in their bedroom.

"I know." He sat on the side of the bed and faced the window. "It's fine."

"It's not fine if you won't even look at me."

He rested his head in his hands suddenly feeling tired and not knowing why.

"I don't understand…" Her voice died away and he heard her footsteps retreat. "Okay, I'll leave you alone. I'll sleep with Syrah tonight then and—"

He reached her before she could get to the door. He swung her into the circle of his arms and held her tenderly. "I'm sorry," he whispered into her hair. "I didn't mean to shout and I'm glad you're home safe."

"Your heart's pounding."

"Hmm."

She looked up at him. "Kenneth?"

He heard a world of questions in her voice, but he wasn't ready for them yet. He held her tighter and said in a teasing tone, "Why won't you leave your husband and be with me? Your husband's an idiot sometimes."

Jessie tapped his chest with her forefinger. "I won't leave my husband because I love him too much. And he needs me."

Kenneth lifted a brow in surprise. "He needs you?"

"Yes, so he can stop pretending." She drew away from him. "What's wrong? And don't act like you don't know what I'm saying. You're free now, you don't have to pretend anymore, remember?"

"I want Christmas to be perfect."

"Christmas will be wonderful, okay? What's with you and Syrah recently?" she asked. "You don't have to be Mr. Perfect anymore. We've got our schedule planned from Christmas to New Years' with family and friends. Even if things go wrong it won't matter because it will be one of many memories we'll get to share. I don't know why she thought we needed the protection of those stones."

***

On Christmas Eve, they sat in front of the fireplace, the tree lit and the remnants of the sugar cookies and eggnog they'd enjoyed set to the side. Jessie told him and Syrah tales of when she and her sisters would wait up for Father Christmas. She made Syrah laugh and Kenneth watched them, wondering why he still felt so tired instead of happy. It was Christmas Eve.

Stop pretending, Jessie had told him. *You must trust her with everything*, Teresa had said. And she was right. Jessie was the one person he could be real with.

He needed to be honest. He hadn't really been afraid of her ignoring him regarding the stones, or getting killed. Those fears gave him a shield against what truly scared him, that the Christmas he was hoping for would be out of reach.

He worried that he wouldn't feel as he was supposed to. He'd never found Christmas a magical season. He'd never had a chance to believe in Father Christmas. All his life, he'd smiled his way through the season to please others, but he always felt like a fraud because the presents and the lights never warmed his heart. And he knew the truth would disappoint her. But pretending had become too much of a burden.

He kissed Syrah goodnight before she went off to bed, then Kenneth sat alone with Jessie on the couch.

He realized that he hoped by making Syrah and Jessie happy, and that their joy would somehow stir something in him. That he'd feel what the season was about. He didn't want to tell her that every song left him feeling numb and he felt exhausted under the weight of a cheer he didn't feel. "I've never liked Christmas. I always lie and say I do, but…"

She looped her fingers through his and he gained strength in her touch. "Go on."

"When I first saw those stones, I didn't know why they bothered me so much, but then I remembered one Christmas when my father got drunk and smashed the ornaments on our tree. I don't know how old I was but I remember how they sparkled even as they shattered and scattered on the ground." He briefly shut his eyes. "I can't feel Christmas. The importance of it…. I can't…I can't feel it. I know I'm supposed to be ecstatic."

"You don't have to be."

"And there's this memory that keeps trying to come back."

"Why won't you let it?"

He rested his head back. "Because I don't want to."

"Maybe you need to."

He turned to her, his eyes clinging to hers. "Most of my memories hurt."

"I know." She patted her lap. "And you don't have to fight them alone anymore, you have me."

A smile softened his mouth. "Are you inviting me to sit on your lap like a good little boy?"

She frowned. "No, I was offering you a place to rest your head." She began to stand. "But if you're not interested—"

He pulled her down. "You know I am," he said in a deep voice.

Kenneth took a deep breath and laid his head down, letting himself surrender to the memory that had been haunting him, trying to become fully formed in his mind. He drifted to sleep, remembering another Christmas blanketed in white.

White was everywhere. White like snow, except he saw the white of a doctor's lab coat, the nurse's shoes, the hospital walls and floors. There were paintings of cartoon characters in the halls, but he didn't recognize most of them because he didn't get to watch TV much. He remembered a white pillow and a metal bed and the sound of holiday music floating from somewhere. And he remembered making a wish…

A wish he'd forgotten about.

He opened his eyes and although it was still dark, the darkness that had seized his soul was gone. He felt his numbness fade and it hurt, but he welcomed the pain because at least he could feel, and the anger and restlessness had gone. He sat up and looked around the room in renewed wonder. He saw the brilliant lights on the tree, the red flashing flames of the fire, but most of all, he saw a home. His home. The one he shared with his daughter who was safe in her room. The one he shared with his wife who'd fight his battles with him.

For the first time in years, he let himself remember the wish of a little boy, spending the holidays in the hospital after a beating, and his wish for a new family that loved him no matter what.

Stop pretending.

He didn't have to pretend anymore.

"Kenneth, are you okay?" Jessie asked him.

He turned to her, the fire glow caressing her brown skin. "Yes," he said, the truth of his words filling him with joy. "Yes," he said again, then stood pulling her up with him. He walked to the window and looked outside at the white snow as it lay under the gaze of the moonlight. He no longer hated the sight. Instead, he saw a whole new beginning.

As they stood by the window, he told her about his memory. His voice was soft as he spoke, his arms wrapped around her waist. She didn't speak, just listened as she rested her back against his chest.

When he was through, he took a deep breath. "You're right," he said. "It will be a wonderful Christmas."

Every Christmas before had been a disappointment to him, but not this one. This one would be like no other. One he'd remember for the rest of his life. Not because it was perfect, but because his long ago wish had finally come true.

If you enjoyed *The Perfect Christmas* don't miss Kenneth and Jessie's romance in *The Sapphire Pendant.*

A Song to Remember

Bitterness didn't have a taste. It had a smell and it smelled like cigarette ashes and vintage wine. To her, bitterness wasn't roads not taken, it was too many options and not enough time. It was facing mortality with grim surrender.

Sharon Burnell sat alone in her dressing room, the soft patter of snow tapping against the window. The sight was a rare treat for Washington DC. It had been a rather warm December and few expected to see snow until January and certainly not in time for Christmas.

She knew she shouldn't have been there. She should be at home, resting in the quiet solitude of her apartment. But she'd returned to the theater for something—a scarf or an earring, she didn't remember what. Now it didn't matter. All that mattered was the silence. A silence filled with bitterness. Only hours before she'd been bedecked in jewels and silk, but that was now gone as was the audience and the unknown faces behind the scenes. The theater lay empty and silent, except for the guards and the cleaning crew.

As she sat in her dressing room, she caught a glimpse of herself in the mirror and sighed. The stage makeup she'd worn had been wiped clean from her face, leaving it bare. She had an ordinary face. A face that seemed, with each day, to grow more familiar to her, though she didn't know why. There was no one in her family who had a nose that was quite like hers or a mouth that was a little crooked. Her walnut skin was still smooth though she saw some sagging around the edges of a jaw that used to be more angular, a neck that had been more regal.

She was at that lonely, unremarkable age when she was too old to live and too young to die.

Tonight, as she'd performed, she felt like a fraud. An imposter. What once had filled her with joy, left her empty. The applause no longer fed her spirit as it once had. The accolades meant nothing. They said she was one of the greatest, but she didn't think so. Her voice wasn't what it had once been. She hadn't reached the notes with the same power and verve. When had her life become worn floorboards and petulant conductors? When had a stage ceased to delight her? Tonight, when she'd looked at the stage, instead of seeing the lush Riviera she only saw broad paint strokes that were supposed to be waves.

Where had the magic gone? The mystery and the majesty of music had escaped her, but she didn't know when or how she'd allowed it to slip from her grasp. But it had left her desolate like a lover whose heart had grown cold.

She was no longer a young darling, but far from being a legend. Again, too young for that, but too old to be one of the fresh young things now flooding stages and concert halls around the globe.

Oh how she wished to see the magic again. But once you know how magic is done, can you ever see it again? She closed her eyes against tears.

When she opened them, she saw a young girl of about fourteen wearing outdated clothes from the 60s, standing on the other side of the room.

A young girl who looked familiar.

Sharon jumped to her feet. "What are you doing here?" she demanded.

But the young girl didn't hear her. Instead, she walked around the room, her face filled with wonder. "It's so beautiful. Oh, how I'd love to have my own dressing room and sing in a theater like this one day," she said.

Sharon's heart raced. Why didn't the young girl see her and why did her face and voice seem so familiar?

"Come on, you don't recognize yourself?" an amused female voice said.

Sharon screamed and glanced around the room not knowing where the voice had come from. The young girl walked past Sharon, still not seeing her or hearing anything. Goose bumps scattered up and down Sharon's arms as a familiar scent lingered.

"What's going on?" She held the side of her head. "Am I having a stroke?"

"You're not having a stroke, Sharon," the voice said. "Must you always be so dramatic?" She hurried over to a corner and her gaze darted around the room, searching for the source

of the voice, but she didn't see anything. "Who are you?"

"No," the voice said. "That's not the question you need answered. The real question is, Who is she?"

Sharon looked again at the young girl who now sat in her chair and pretended to put on makeup. She then understood why she looked so familiar. She was looking at herself. The girl she'd been many years ago.

Soon the dressing room fell away and she saw her old bedroom—a stack of vinyl records she'd bought, although they didn't own a record player, a black and white photo of her friend from Liverpool; she smelled the scent of eggs and chips wafting from the kitchen. Outside, a drizzly grey rain soaked the city of Manchester, England, and the young girl stood by the window staring down at one of the records she couldn't listen to.

Sharon felt tears touch her eyes remembering that moment and noticing the welt on her arm where her grandfather had struck her with a switch because he thought she was trying to poison him. Her parents didn't want him to go into a nursing home, although caring for him had become more difficult. Her parents had taken her out of school so they could work and she had to look after him. Music helped her endure the confinement. At least they had a radio and at night she'd hold the dial just right so she could get to listen to her favorite station.

Having a piano helped too. Through the music she created on the black and white keys, she was transported to the hot streets of New York City and to the classical dance halls of Vienna. Music transported her grandfather too, because when she sang with him, he was like his old self. He would smile and dance and when she sang his favorite tunes it was as if years were erased from his face and his mind became clear. *If only she could sing forever.*

The young girl looked straight at Sharon, as if she could see her. And Sharon's heart began to race. Would she scream? Call the police? But the young girl didn't look surprised. "I didn't think you'd come back," she said, setting the record down on her bed.

"You mean I've been here before?"

The young girl frowned. "Yea, you don't remember?"

No, but now she started to understand why the mature face she'd seen in the mirror had felt so familiar to her. She'd seen it before as her younger self. "Hmm."

"Did you really mean what you said before?"

Oh no. What had she said? Sharon thought in a panic then the words came to her. *If you keep the magic alive, it will never leave you, but if you forget you will wither and die.* Why had she said that? But even as she asked herself the question, she knew the answer. It was a warning. She'd allowed herself to forget the magic. What music had once meant to her. Like the memories stolen from her grandfather, she'd quietly lost what had made her whole. She couldn't let herself do it again, this was her second chance. "Yes," she said with a desperate fervor looking at the young face before her and seeing it wasn't the smooth skin or the lack of years that would later catapult her into her long career, it would be her passion. A passion that would send her around the world, to marvel at the five languages she'd learn to speak, gasp at the sight of tears rolling down her parents' faces when she sang in Carnegie Hall. A passion she must continue to let burn.

She hadn't tended to it. She'd taken it for granted, until slowly it had burned out.

"Sharon!" her grandfather called and she remembered that her name was one of the few he still remembered. Her younger self went to where he sat in the living room. He didn't see the older version.

"Ask him to play something," Sharon told her younger self.

And the young girl did. The older man shuffled to the piano, but once he sat down, his back straightened, his arms and fingers flexed and as he played all the years fell away. Sharon remembered the tune and sang along and her younger self joined her.

And as the magic rained down around them, tears of shame touched her eyes. She felt ashamed by how easily she'd allowed herself to forget how fortunate she was, how far she'd come, how much she'd let herself forget, and how much she needed to remember.

Soon the pair fazed away and she sat in the audience and saw herself on stage in one of her performances ten years ago and although she didn't see a legend or an ingénue, she saw someone more radiant. She saw a woman in love. In love with the magic that surrounded her as the music soared through the room, flowing through her and touching the hearts of those around her. And behind her, she saw the waves instead of the brushstrokes; she saw the horizon and could hear the seagulls. The scenery came alive.

Her breath caught when the woman performing, looked at her—and she felt the connection. She could hear her urgent plea 'Never forget me'.

She understood that request. She would never forget why she sang. She sang for the girl growing up in a small flat in Manchester who dreamed of a different life. She sang for the woman who couldn't believe where her life had taken her. She sang for her grandfather who first showed her the magic, by playing the piano and teaching her show tunes. Sharon nodded, making a promise not to get caught up in the criticisms, the trinkets of fame and fortune or her own ego. She was there to serve the music.

The woman seemed to smile and finished her song to thunderous applause.

Silence soon descended and Sharon found herself standing in the corner of her dressing room again, but the scent of bitterness was gone.

And she knew she'd never smell it again. The magic had returned.

No, she realized as she gathered her things to face the snowy weather outside, a new sense of joy bubbling inside, it had never left.

A Mother's Day Wish

"We don't need you. We have a lawn service to take care of things," Beth Armstrong said looking at the lanky fifteen year old who'd asked to mow her lawn. She was surprised he'd even offered. He was a Bailey after all and everyone knew the Baileys were a lazy bunch. The only effort his father extended was to find a woman and get his pants down or open a bottle and fill his belly with liquor. People knew better than to hire him because he'd never show up, but would always come up with an excuse as to why. Just like his father before him. Even his great-grandfather had a notorious reputation back in Trinidad. He'd been a man not to be trusted. Beth didn't expect young Cole Bailey to be much different. He was a good looking young man with dark lashes and brows, but the Bailey men always were.

She hardened her heart against the look of disappointment that dimmed Cole's light brown eyes and turned the corners of his mouth down. She couldn't bend. She wouldn't. People had been trying to help the Baileys for years and nothing ever worked. She gripped the door handle, stiffened her spine and let a slight, polite smile touch her lips. "I'm sorry. Goodbye and good day."

"Good day," Cole said not meaning a word. He forced a smile then turned. It didn't feel like a good day but that was all he'd been forced to hear. The Armstrong house had been his last stop. Nobody would hire him. He'd offered lawn care, window washing, spider web cleaning and painting, but he always got a polite 'good day' and a door in his face. He knew the people of Hamsford didn't want a Bailey inside their homes, but he'd hoped they'd at least let him help outside with the grunt work. Wasn't he good enough for that? None of the local shop owners would give him work, his father and grandfather's reputations always proceeded him. But he wasn't his father or grandfather.

Unfortunately, no one would give him the chance to prove it. And he needed a break. He needed to make money to help his family, especially his younger sisters who deserved more than what they were getting—a fridge that was usually empty and a cramped, dank apartment. His parents were already two months late on the rent. Cole knew the rent was really six months overdue, but his father had managed to bargain it down to two months since he was sleeping with the landlord's wife and she'd somehow persuaded her husband to lower what was owed. Cole didn't know how long the arrangement would last, since his father never stuck with anyone or anything long. He wanted to make sure he had enough money to take care of the family in case something went wrong, which it usually did.

Yes, his sisters deserved better. Just thinking of them made him smile. They were the only people in town who loved and looked up to him. They were so sweet and smart. He remembered when he'd gone to the church charity looking for clothes he'd picked up an old stain glass kit for his thirteen year old sister, Angela. She made amazing art with it, which he put up near the windows giving their gloomy place some beauty as it cast rainbows on the walls and floor. He wanted to get her some more tools and pay for a school trip to an art gallery in two months. Then there was his shy little sister, Grace, who needed braces. She was ten and her teeth were growing in crooked. Kids were already making fun of her and she had no friends.

Not that his parents noticed. His mother was always in a foul mood, angry that she'd ended up marrying a 'good for nothing Bailey' and getting 'good for nothing children.' His father was hardly around but nobody missed him anyway.

Cole slowly walked down the path that cut through the Armstrong's manicured lawn trying to think of another way to make money when he saw an older woman coming towards him carrying heavy bags. He rushed up to her. "Let me help you," he said half expecting her to refuse. People didn't let Baileys help them.

"Oh thank you," she said offering him a bright smile of relief. "I bought more than I should have."

Cole stopped and stared at her for a moment in amazement. She'd smiled at him. Not a fake distant smile, but a real genuine one. He'd never had that before. He took her bags even more eager to please her just to get her to smile at him again. She had a nice round face, sparkling eyes, warm brown skin and grey hair. If he had a grandmother he'd want one to be just like her. He helped her carry her bags to the door, wishing he could help her with something else.

"Thank you young man," she said taking her keys out of her handbag.

"My pleasure," he said liking the soft island lilt of her words.

"What's your name?"

Suddenly, the door swung open, cutting off his reply. "Mother," Beth said in an urgent rush. "Are you okay?"

"I'm perfectly fine," she said startled. "This young man—"

Beth snatched the bags from Cole and anxiously peered inside. "You'd better check to make sure everything is here. Baileys have sticky fingers."

The woman shot her daughter a glance of annoyance. "Of course everything is there. I didn't raise you to be facety like this."

Beth sent Cole a look of suspicion. "Why are you back here? I told you we can't use you."

"He was helping me."

Beth set the bags aside and pulled money from her purse. She held out a five dollar bill and waved it at him with impatience."Fine you can go now."

Cole took a step back, trying to take rein on his temper. He wanted to take the five dollars and ram it in her mouth. He could show her how much of a sticky fingered no good Bailey he could be. Instead he gripped his hands into fists. "I'm gone."

"Wait," the older woman said grabbing his sleeve. "What did you come for?"

"To mow the lawn," Beth said.

Her mother stared at her, raising her eyebrows. "Is this a puppet show? I ask him a question and you answer?"

"No, mother but—"

"Then keep your mouth shut 'til I ask you to open it again." She turned her attention to Cole. "Come inside. I want to talk to you." Before her daughter could protest the woman stepped past her and said, "Put the kettle on. I'm thirsty." She ignored the stunned silence that followed her request and headed for the kitchen.

Cole hesitated then followed. He'd never been inside such a fine house before. He gaped at the rose colored wallpaper and polished wooden floors. There wasn't a cockroach in sight. When he passed the family room he quickly peeked inside and saw Mr. Armstrong standing near the fireplace and his son, Grant, reading a book. He knew Grant from school, not personally, but from a distance and by reputation. Grant always had a crowd of admirers around him since he was a track star and talented musician. Cole was too in awe to notice the frown on Grant's face when he saw him. He hurried to the kitchen then halted at the sight of how large it was. His entire apartment could fit inside it.

"Sit down," the woman said getting some Jamaican bun and cheese out of the refrigerator. She set them on the table.

He sat, rubbing his hands together under the table. "Yes, Mother Armstrong."

"No," she said with a laugh. "I'm not an Armstrong. That's my daughter's married name. Just call me Ms. Hetty."

"Hey Bailey," a voice said behind him. He turned and saw Grant standing in the doorway, a look of annoyance on his face. "What are you doing here?"

Cole opened his mouth to reply, but Hetty beat him to it. "We're having a private conservation. You can talk to him later."

Grant scowled then stormed away.

"So you do lawn care?" Hetty asked.

"Yes ma'am," he said. He'd tried to join a landscaping crew but no one would hire him. However, he'd watched them work and picked up skills. He didn't have the equipment, but knew how they worked.

"What else can you do?"

Beth came into the kitchen and filled the kettle at the sink.

"Polish silver," he said.

She set the kettle on the stove and mumbled, "And steal it too."

Cole shifted in his seat, wanting to defend himself but knowing he couldn't.

"Go on," Hetty urged.

"I can clean spider webs."

Beth rested a hand on her hip. "You think I'd allow spiders to build webs in my house? My house is spotless."

"I didn't mean to offend."

"You might as well say you'd kill mice too."

"I can if you need me too."

Beth gasped. "You cheeky little—"

"Quiet, Beth," her mother interrupted.

She pointed at Cole. "Did you just hear what he said? He sits in my home and implies that we have mice!"

"Be quiet."

"But—"

Hetty turned to her daughter. "Have you forgotten that I'm still your mother? I said keep your mouth shut and I mean it. I can still box your ears and I'll make it your mouth if I have to." She turned back to Cole. "Go on."

He cleared his throat. "I'm good at fixing things."

"Anything in particular?"

"Anything you ask me to."

Hetty nodded. "Good I have a task for you. I have a lawn swing that needs to be fixed. Can you do that?"

"Yes."

"How much?" Cole gave her a price and she shook her head. "Too high."

Cole rubbed his hands and swallowed. He didn't want to lose her business, but he also didn't want to admit that he didn't even own a hammer or screwdriver. He needed money to buy tools. "I'll also paint the trim if you like."

"The price is still too high."

He lowered his gaze. *Think Bailey. You need this job.* He knew what his father would do. He'd try to sweet talk her, but he was no good at that. He liked to be honest. He sighed he hoped that wouldn't be a mistake. "I can lower the price if you'd allow me to use your tools."

Beth opened her mouth then quickly closed it, remembering her mother's threat.

"How much?" Hetty asked.

He gave her another price.

Hetty smiled and held out her hand. "Agreed. Come back tomorrow after ten."

Cole shook her hand, careful not to pump it too hard. He really wanted to give her a big hug. He'd made her smile and now had a job. He grinned back. "I will. Good day," he said, meaning every word.

***

At dinner Beth bristled with outrage. "You won't believe what Mother did today. She hired a Bailey."

Arthur Armstrong looked at his mother-in-law, who was calmly eating her dinner, then at the pinched face of his wife. His three sons waited to see how he would handle the situation. He chose to proceed with caution. "To do what?"

"Does it matter?"

"I'm curious."

"Fix the lawn swing."

"Why didn't you say so, Mother? I could have gotten it fixed for you."

Hetty did not raise her gaze from the curried trout and creamy scalloped potatoes on her plate. "On three occasions I asked but no one listened. I was tired of waiting."

"Mother," he said in a soft patronizing tone. "You're new to this place so you don't know the people. Some of them you just can't trust."

"Exactly," Beth said. "The Bailey men are lazy, worthless men. What will people think? You don't know what you've done."

"I know exactly what I've done. I gave a young man a chance," Hetty said.

"But he's a—"

"He's not his father. Let him prove himself."

Grant touched her shoulder. "I'll fix it for you, Gran."

Hetty repressed a shudder. It wasn't good to not like one's own flesh and blood but she didn't take to her grandson. She found him to be as slick as palm oil. After her husband's death she'd looked forward to moving in with her daughter's family, but the move hadn't been as peaceful as she'd hoped. Her daughter was constantly correcting her, her son-in-law ignored her and her grand-children barely noticed her. She'd carried heavy shopping bags before without anyone caring. To everyone she was just an invisible old woman. That young Bailey boy had been the first to take any notice. To really make her feel as if she mattered, not to feel as if she were just a burden or obligation. She had plenty of money, because she and her husband had been savvy with their finances, and could go to a residential facility, but she didn't want to be around just old people. But being around the younger generations wasn't much fun either. At times she considered moving to the cottage she and her husband still owned in New York and had used as a holiday house, but it would be lonely there.

"I've already hired Cole," Hetty said. "And I plan to keep my word."

"But—"

"I'm a grown woman and I've made up my mind. This has nothing to do with any of you."

***

That evening Hetty took out an old photograph and sat on her bed staring at the faded image. It was a picture of her cousin Lenny, a fine looking young man who'd been shot and killed in an armed robbery bust when the police mistook him for one of the assailants. She remembered returning to Trinidad to attend his funeral. She let her finger trail over his smiling happy face. No one had given him a chance. No one had taken the time to look past his poor grades and background to see what a hardworking young man he was. She remembered how he could make you smile when you wanted to cry and how he never felt sorry for himself. Cole somehow reminded her of him. Unlike Lenny, she would make sure he was given an opportunity to prove himself. But she knew helping Cole wasn't just for him, it was for her. She glanced around her crowded bedroom filled with stuff she could afford, but didn't need. It offered her no comfort. She was restless. She had done her child-drearing and had worked most of her life. She'd waited all her life for these days of leisure, but she was bored. She wanted to do something. She wanted a reason to live. Cole had not only noticed her, he'd made her feel useful. He'd made her feel viable again.

***

Cole arrived the next day at ten on the dot. Hetty sat in a lawn chair and watched him work. He was a good worker. Skinnier than he should be but strong. He told her about his sisters. They laughed together that Saturday like two kids getting to know each other and shared a lunch of spicy chicken patties and talked about their frustrations.

"No one will give me a chance," Cole said as they finished their meal.

"I did and I know others will too."

"I really want to thank you."

Hetty waved his thanks aside. "It's not a big issue. I'm glad you could help me and respect me." She sighed. "Sometimes my family treats me as if I were two years old."

"I wish I could take you home with me," Cole said. "I'd let you do whatever you wanted."

"Where do you live?"

Cole shook his head. "It's not good enough for you." He wondered if he'd ever have a place good enough for her to visit. Baileys had never owned anything. But he pushed the thought away and finished fixing her swing. Hetty giggled with delight when it was finished and immediately tried it out. She then gave him another task and soon he was a regular at the Armstrong house. To his surprise, word quickly spread and he was able to get other small jobs around town. But no job compared to working for Ms. Hetty, Cole thought as he dug up a patch of dirt she wanted to use as a herb garden. She was one of the most wonderful women he'd ever met: Smart and pretty and sweet and he loved her.

He'd given her a card for Mother's Day wishing he could spend every Mother's Day with her and treat her and his sisters to brunch like other families did. His mother hated Mother's Day and didn't like cards. She said they were just expensive pieces of paper unless there was money inside. But not Ms. Hetty. When Cole had given her his card—he'd wanted to get her perfume or flowers but a card was all he could afford—she'd given him one of her beaming smiles and held the card close as if he'd given her a treasure. Even though her family had treated her to buffet and gifts of scarves and jewelry she made him feel that his gift was just as important. And that night he wished he could always make her smile and imagined spending every holiday with her from New Year's Day to Christmas. He wished he could rescue her somehow. He hated to know she was unhappy living with her family. He knew how she felt, but he didn't know what he could do. He was close to raising enough money for Angela's school trip and with more jobs he could raise enough for Grace, but helping Ms. Hetty would take a miracle. At least he was glad that luck was finally on his side.

***

Grant watched Cole from his bedroom window with seething anger. Why was his grandmother paying attention to that dirty old Bailey? His friends were already ribbing him about it. Bailey was making him a laughing stock. He was the one who was supposed to shine. He was the track star and musician, but his grandmother barely took notice of him. What was so important about a stupid swing anyway? And why did she keep having to have him come back? Bailey almost acted like he belonged there, but he didn't. Hell, he could even sense his parents starting to like him and his two brothers had once asked Bailey to join them for a soccer game. He hated Cole Bailey. He should know his place.

That night Grant went into the garden and unscrewed a major hinge on the swing. He smiled as he imagined the havoc he'd just created. Now Bailey would get what he deserved.

***

Hetty loved to sit outside on late spring evenings. She was so happy that she now had a beautiful swing to sit in. Outside she felt close to Lenny and her husband and no longer thought of them with pain. Her heart had a new resident. Cole had filled her life with laughter and joy. She hoped to one day meet Cole's sisters since he talked so fondly about them. She sat on her swing and swayed back and forth then she heard a snap and the swing came crashing down. Shooting pain followed. She cried out as hot tears filled her eyes.

Beth rushed to her. "Mother!" She turned to her husband who'd followed close behind and said, "Call an ambulance."

Minutes later Hetty was taken to the hospital where they discovered she'd broken her hip. Infection quickly set in and for days Hetty was gravely ill, but to the relief of her family she pulled through.

Cole, however, soon found his world shattered. Word quickly spread about his poor workmanship and soon he was being called a 'no good Bailey' again and what little work he'd been able to get dried up.

"So typical," his mother said as he cleared up the fast food dinner he'd bought with money he'd saved. She sniffed in disgust. "You Bailey men always screw up a good thing."

"I know I fixed it right," Cole said, wishing there had been leftovers for tomorrow night's dinner. The greasy chicken meal was nothing like the baked plantain and jerk chicken Ms. Hetty had once treated him to, but it was still food.

His mother rested back in her chair, putting her feet on the table. Her boots added to the many scratches that were already there. "Then why did it break nearly killing the old woman?"

Cole swallowed feeling a little ill. "I don't know, but I didn't make a mistake. I tested it myself and I'm heavier than Ms. Hetty. I would never do anything to hurt her."

"Just take responsibility," Angela said. "Go to the hospital and ask for forgiveness."

He shook his head. "I can't face her."

"I thought she was your friend," his youngest sister, Grace, said.

Cole blinked back tears. She was and that was why he couldn't face her. He didn't care what anyone else thought of him, but if she thought he was a 'good for nothing' Bailey he couldn't handle it.

"You have to visit her," Angela insisted.

He hung his head. He knew he was disappointing them. He'd disappointed everyone. "Leave me alone." He turned wishing there was somewhere to hide. Unfortunately, there was nowhere to go to get away, so he went into the stairwell. He collapsed onto one of the steps, covered his face and cried. He loved Ms. Hetty and wished he was in the hospital instead of her. He wished he could take all her pain away, especially since he was the cause. He was a 'no good Bailey' who deserved to die. His mother was right. He was a screw up. He was no different than the rest of the Baileys. Cole quickly wiped his eyes, when he heard footsteps, and turned his face to the wall.

Angela sat beside him and lightly rested a hand on his shoulder. "You have to go see her. "

He kept his face turned and shook his head.

"I want you to give her something."

Cole let his shoulders droop then slowly looked at his sister and saw that she held a small stain glass project in her hand.

"It can't be fun being stuck in a hospital, this will brighten it up for her."

Cole sighed, taking the stain glass. It was a picture of a garden. He was so close to making their lives better and he'd failed. There would be no school trip or braces, but he'd at least do this for her.

***

The next day, he dressed in his best suit. When his mother saw him she laughed. "You're going to a damn hospital not a funeral."

"I want to look my best."

"If you were your father, I'd wonder if you wanted to sweet talk a nurse."

Cole arranged his tie. "No."

"I'm surprised you haven't knocked up a girl yet, but you're still young so there's still time."

"I'm not Dad."

"You better not do that or you're out."

He nodded. He'd heard that since he was five. It wasn't that he wasn't interested in girls, but he had to take care of his family first. And now he had to help Ms. Hetty.

She helped straighten his tie. "Not that it will matter. No matter how fine you look you'll never be one of them."

"I'm not trying to be."

"Then why are you acting as if you're meeting the damn queen or something?"

He knew his mother wouldn't understand, but he wanted to look his best for Ms. Hetty. He wanted to let her know how sorry he was and tell her he would find a way to make things up to her. He took Angela's wrapped gift and left the apartment.

***

Grant met him outside the door to Hetty's hospital room. His gaze swept Cole's worn suit and his mouth quirked in a sneer. "What are you? The undertaker?"

"I came to see Ms. Hetty."

"Sorry. It's family only," he said.

"I just have to give her something."

Grant held out his hand. "I'll give it to her."

"No."

Grant lowered his voice and narrowed his eyes. "Listen Bailey, I can make your life even more miserable than it is now so you'd better just take my advice and leave."

"I'm not afraid of you."

"That's your mistake. I can—"

"I don't care. I want to see Ms. Hetty."

"Is that Cole?" Hetty called out. "Is that you, my dear?"

"Yes, ma'am," he said boldly meeting Grant's glare. "It's me."

"Are you waiting for an invitation? Come on in."

Cole shoved past Grant.

"There's a hole in your suit," Grant said.

Cole ignored him and walked into the room. Hetty had her own private room. It was filled with flowers. He thought of Angela's gift and knew that it couldn't compete with the grander surrounding him. "I'm so sorry," he said in a rush. "I was sure everything was secure."

"What no hug?" Hetty said lifting her arms out to him.

He gently hugged her. She smelled like lilacs and felt as warm as a summer morning.

"Be careful," Beth snapped, coming into the room. "You've done enough damage. I'm surprised you can show your face."

"I'm sorry, Mrs. Armstrong. I was sure—"

"What have you brought for me?" Hetty said eyeing the package under his arm.

"It's from my sister Angela. She thought you might like it."

"Next time tell her to come." Hetty opened the package then gasped at the item inside. "It's beautiful."

Beth walked over to take a look. "Your sister made this herself?"

Cole nodded with pride. "Yes ma'am."

"We have to put it up." Hetty pointed to the window. "Rest it there so the sunlight can filter through."

Cole did just that and then they all stared at it.

"Hetty," a voice called from the doorway then an elegantly dressed woman walked into the room. "You're always causing trouble little sister." The woman stopped and stared at the stain glass. "Oh, where did you get this?"

"It's a gift," Hetty said. She gestured to Cole. "His sister makes them."

"How much?" the woman asked, picking it up to take a closer look.

Hetty gave a reply that left Cole speechless.

"Very well. I'd like to order one. You know that Todd is looking for a student to mentor. Do you think your sister would be interested?" she asked Cole.

"Yes ma'am."

She pulled out her card. "Have her call me."

Cole stared at the card. No one had ever given him their card before. "Yes ma'am."

Grant stood near the door and watched the scene wanting to punch something. This wasn't how it was supposed to be. They were supposed to hate him. "Why are you helping his sister?" he said. "He's the reason you're in here."

"And I forgive him," Hetty said.

"You could have died."

"But I didn't and I think it was meant to be."

Grant widened his eyes incredulous."Meant to be?"

"Yes, " she said with a bright smile. "All because of the great man above. If I hadn't broken my hip, I wouldn't be here and then Cole's sister wouldn't have given me this picture and my sister wouldn't have seen it and then consider recommending her to Todd. Yes. It's all meant to be. God at work."

"But it wasn't God. I was—" Grant stopped before he implicated himself.

Hetty met his eyes with a keen intelligence that sent a shiver through him. "You were what?"

Grant shook his head, as a trickle of sweat slid down his back. "Nothing. I just think—"

Hetty clapped her hands. "I just had an idea." She turned to Cole. "If my sister has anything to do with it, Angela will be accepted into Todd's program. He's my sister's ex-husband and has an art studio in New York where he mentors aspiring young artists. Angela is very talented and I know he'd enjoy working with her. She would be able to learn and grow her skills while also earning money. "Hetty continued when she saw Cole's hesitation. "I have a house there that I'd love to use again. My husband and I used to go there for vacations. Your sister could live there and she'll need someone to be there with her. I've always wanted to live there but not by myself. I could lookout for her. But we'd need someone to help around the house. Would you like to go too?"

"Oh yes, but..." His words fell away.

"But what?"

"I have another sister."

"There are good schools there. She can come too."

"Mother," Beth said stunned. "What are you saying?"

"'I've got a lot of life left in me and I'm not ready to be put out to pasture. I'm moving."

"I thought you were happy with us. And we can take care of you."

"That's the problem. I don't need you to."

"But these three Bailey kids will—"

"Be the greatest gift to me," she finished.

"Their parents—"

Hetty brushed her concerns aside with a wave of her hand. "I'll make it worth their while."

And she did. Mrs. Bailey was relieved to see her children go so she could have another life. Mr. Bailey wasn't around to argue. Angela was accepted into Todd's exclusive mentorship program, Grace got her braces and enrolled in a private school nearby and Cole felt glad he'd managed to get the life his sisters deserved, leaving the Bailey reputation far behind.

And as they sat in their little house one fall afternoon, Cole thought back to the night he'd imagined spending every holiday with Ms. Hetty and he grinned knowing his Mother's Day wish had come true.

A Fortunate Mistake

The phone call shattered a beautiful crying fit at 3 a.m. on Christmas Eve. Marina Durosomo had gone through an entire box of tissues and blown her nose until it hurt and her red rimmed eyes were dry when the piercing of the phone invaded her quiet apartment. She wanted to ignore it, to continue to drown in her misery and the stinging critique of her now closed bakery that continued to torment her, but the insistent ringing wouldn't stop. Who could be calling her now? She didn't want to hear more bad news. She reluctantly reached for the phone, slow enough to hope that by the time she picked up, the person on the other end would hang up.

"Hello?" she said.

"Did I wake you?"

Marina wiped her eyes, recognizing her mother's voice. She was good at asking questions that didn't need an answer. If she said 'yes', her mother would apologize but not really mean it. If she said 'no', her mother would ask what was wrong and she didn't want to tell her. "I'm fine."

"You sound like you're coming down with a cold."

"I'm fine," she repeated, tossing her empty box of tissues into the recycling bin.

"You don't sound—"

"Mom, what's wrong?"

"I need you to pick up Aunty Helen."

"Aunty who?"

"That's her English name. You won't remember her real one. Besides, you don't know her. She's the mother of a good friend of ours."

Because her mother had about twenty 'good friends' Marina didn't even try to make the connection. It wasn't unusual to have unexpected visitors arrive from Nigeria. They treated their family like a taxi and hotel service, but her mother and father were steeped in the tradition of hospitality and didn't want anything negative said about them back home, even though an ocean separated them. "Okay when will she be here?"

"She's arriving at four-thirty."

"This morning?"

"Yes, why else would I be calling you now? You have an hour and a half to get ready and be over there."

Her mother made it sound so sensible. "Why me?"

"She's coming in at BWI. You're closer to the airport and I have to go to work."

"I work too."

Her mother's responding silence was eloquent. She used to work. She used to have a business she was proud of, but that was all over now. All because of a major recession and a business partner who'd embezzled her funds and disappeared. But no, the truth was her business hadn't failed. She had. There were other bakeries that were flourishing, but the critique had shown a light on all her fears. She just wasn't good enough. Her mother had told her the bakery was a foolish dream, that she should have tried for something more sensible. Her mother would never say 'I told you so', but she didn't have to. Now she would be chauffer to some stranger. This was her punishment. She hated the holidays. Every year they seemed to show her how far she was from the life she wanted. It highlighted another year of grasping for something out of reach.

"What's her flight number?" Marina asked to fill the silence and resigned to her fate.

Her mother told her.

"Can't Wale go?"

"I can't reach him. Hurry, I don't want her waiting there alone. And this will be good for you."

"Good?"

"Yes, to get out of your apartment."

"Mom, I don't need to hear this right now. I just want to sleep."

"You can sleep all you want after you pick her up and settle her in your place."

"My place?"

"Yes, we'll come and get her in the evening."

Marina looked around her messy apartment—the carpet needed a good vacuum, she could spell her name in the dust. After her career imploded she hadn't cared about her surroundings. She didn't want a guest, she didn't want to pretend to celebrate the holidays, she wanted to disappear, but she didn't have a choice.

"What does she look like?" Marina asked opening her closet.

"She's tiny."

Marina waited. When her mother didn't elaborate she rolled her eyes and sighed. "That's all? A tiny black woman?"

"You'll find her," her mother said with impatience. "She'll be looking for you and you will find each other. You're smart." She hung up.

Marina scowled at the phone then disconnected.

At times she hated being a diligent daughter. She wanted to say "Let her wait." Why did this Aunty, what-was-her-name—Helga? Hettie?—have to wait until now to let them know she was arriving? So inconsiderate. She could have called them when she changed flights in Amsterdam. But Marina had learned to keep her thoughts to herself. She had no husband or children to hide behind and now she couldn't even say she had a business to run. She had no life, so she had to do as she was told.

Chapter Two

Marina stood in the baggage claim area of Baltimore Washington International feeling like a farmer trying to find a particular blade of grass in a field. Although it wasn't as crowded as a midmorning or late afternoon flight, there were still enough people to get lost in. Marina shoved her hands in her gray wool coat and rocked on her heels. She still couldn't remember the blasted woman's name—Herma? Hilda? Helen? Yes, that was it Helen! But recalling her name was just a small victory. She had no idea how she was supposed to find this woman. Aunty Helen a woman she'd never heard of who was the grandmother of some friend's mother.

Marina was about to give up hope and call her mother when she saw a small woman standing near the wall with a large bag. She wore a brightly colored headwrap in a pattern she'd never seen before and a well tailored dress that matched. The woman looked composed, as if standing for a portrait—her eighty some years had been kind to her. She had a certain glow that drew Marina to her. She seemed out of place. That had to be her.

Marina made her way over to the woman, confident she'd found the elusive Aunty Helen. Although she wasn't the only one in regional clothes, she was the only one not properly dressed for the cold December weather. At least others sported long coats or gloves, but she only wore her dress, as if she expected to step out into a nice ninety degree sun.

Marina stopped in front of her and smiled."Aunty Helen?"

The woman smiled and her face seemed to glow.

Marina glanced down at her one bag surprised. She'd never picked up someone with so little luggage. "Is that all that you have? Do you need me to help you get the rest?"

She continued to smile.

Marina inwardly groaned. "Please tell me you speak English."

Her smile grew wider.

She softly swore. Why hadn't her mother told her she didn't speak English? That was rare, but the woman looked past eighty so maybe she hadn't had a chance to learn. Unfortunately, her Yoruba wasn't good. She understood it better than speaking it.

In broken Yoruba she attempted to talk to her. "I'm sorry. I'm not good at this. One?" She held up one finger. "Bag?" She pointed to the bag.

The woman blinked and continued to smile.

Marina glanced in the direction of the baggage area and saw that it was empty. "I'm just going to take that as a yes." She turned back to the woman. Things were starting to become a little eerie. She had the bright, trusting nature of a child.”Do you have anything warm in there?” She pointed to the bag again.

The woman blinked, but her smile faltered.

Marina pointed outside then hugged herself and shivered. “Cold. You'll be cold. You need something warm.” She pointed to the bag again then took the strap. “Can I see?”

The woman released her grip confused.

Marina kneeled and opened the bag. “Please tell me someone had the sense to pack a sweater for you.” But she didn't see anything that would be warm enough. Unfortunately, the airport stores were closed. She took off her coat. She had a knit sweater underneath. “You'll have to wear this,” she said wrapping it around the woman.

Her bright smile returned and she patted Marina on the cheek. Her hand was remarkably soft and gentle.

The kind gesture made Marina feel like crying all over again. At least someone felt that she was doing something right. Even if it was as simple as keeping them warm. “You're welcome,” she said in a brusque tone. She stood. “Come on.”

Chapter Three

Aunty Helen didn't say anything on the drive to Marina's apartment. She stared out at the dark, chilly morning, looking at the bright lights of the highway and the large buildings looming on both sides of the highway. Close to her apartment, Marina stopped at an all-night grocery store and bought another box of tissues and a pair of wool gloves.

When she got back into the car, she rubbed her hands together. "Warm enough?"

Aunty Helen just blinked.

Marina put the gloves in her lap. "You'll need these." She put them on her. "Better?" she said, not expecting a reply and not getting one. Instead Aunty Helen held up her hands, flexed her fingers and smiled.

At home, Marina put Aunty Helen's bag in the hall. She wasn't tired and her guest didn't look so either. Marina mimed holding a bowl and spoon and pretended to eat. "Hungry?" she asked.

Aunty Helen blinked.

She mimed drinking. "Or thirsty?"

The woman blinked again.

Marina sighed. "I'll just give you something okay? And then you can rest on the couch until my mother picks you up and I don't know why I keep talking to you when you don't know what I'm saying."

She put on the kettle for tea then quickly put together a meal of peanut soup she'd recently gotten from her mother.

The woman delve into the meal and again patted her on the cheek, but this time Marina didn't feel like crying. She felt glad she'd been able to make the woman happy. She was clearing up her living room couch to give her a place to nap when her phone rang. She checked the number and sighed when she saw her brother, Wale's, number. "What do you want?"

"To warn you. Mom's upset. You're in big trouble," he said in Yoruba.

"I'm always in trouble," she said in kind.

He laughed then said in English. "Your Yoruba still sucks."

"Shut up, it's not too late for me to give you a lump of coal," she said then hung up the phone, wondering why her brother felt like teasing her. And what could her mother be upset about now? A moment later, her phone rang again. She was about to say something rude when she recognized the number.

"Hi Mom."

"Why didn't you pick up Aunty Helen?" she demanded.

"What do you mean? I did." She looked at the woman sitting in her kitchen. "She's right here. You could have told me that she didn't speak English."

"What are you going on about? She speaks perfect English. She has a degree from Oxford."

Marina rolled her eyes, not caring where the woman received her degree, though her mother did. She was about to ask why that mattered when her mother continued.

"She just called. Your brother had to go get her."

Marina felt her stomach drop. "That doesn't make any sense. I have Aunty Helen right here. She's eating in my kitchen."

"Oh my god. What have you done?"

Marina's heart started to race and her breathing became shallow. Had she failed again? How could that be? "I did what you told me to. I picked up a woman matching Aunty Helen's vague description. I even asked her her name." Marina paused remembering the incident. She hadn't really asked her name. She'd just said "Aunty Helen?' and the woman smiled and she assumed it was her. "Wait a moment." She ran into the kitchen where the woman was cleaning up her soup with a warm slice of bread. Aunty Helen?"

The woman looked up and smiled.

"You are Aunty Helen?" Marina repeated to make sure.

She continued to smile.

Could she have the same name as the other woman?

"Mom, she seems fine."

"Describe her to me."

"She's small and about eighty something. She didn't have the proper clothes for the weather and had only one bag."

"Aunty Helen isn't over sixty."

"Why didn't you tell me that before? You said she was the grandmother of one of your friends."

"Not all of my friends are my age. You know that. You should have been more careful. Why are you getting irritated with me? You're the one who picked up the wrong woman. If she were an old woman I would have said Big Mummy not Aunty. Why don't you pay attention to these things? And you should have known I wouldn't send you to pick up someone who doesn't speak English."

Marina rubbed her forehead. Listening to her mother's criticism but only hearing 'you're a failure, you're a failure, you can't do anything right.' "I don't believe this."

"Give her the phone."

Marina held out the phone to her. "Aunty—uh Big Mummy—my mother wants to talk."

The woman nodded and took the phone. She responded with quick fast replies. Her voice was soft and deep, oddly soothing, but Marina couldn't decipher the meaning. The old woman then handed the phone back.

"Why didn't you give her the phone?" her mother demanded when Marina returned to the phone.

Marina squeezed her eyes shut. "What are you talking about? I just did."

"Is she deaf?"

"No. She spoke to you. I heard her. She didn't answer much, but she did speak. I didn't understand her though. It didn't sound like Yoruba. She spoke, but I didn't understand her."

Her mother paused. "You see her? Is she still there?"

"Yes. Where else would she be?"

"Oh no," her mother said in a frightened tone. "I've heard of this but..."

"What?"

"My dear are you sure you're feeling okay? Have you been eating and sleeping properly?"

"Yes, I'm not crazy."

"Lack of sleep can cause hallucinations."

"I'm not hallucinating."

"Or it could be something worse."

"Like what?"

"You picked up a or bloody hell what's the English name for it? I'm not sure they have one exactly. Oh yes...witch."

Don't be daft, she wanted to say, but bit her lip. Her parents believed in both traditional and native religions. "She's not a—I just made a mistake."

"Maybe you should just go back to sleep. If she's still there then get rid of her as fast as you can. Take her to the police and be careful."

Chapter Four

Marina took her new arrival to the police station. "I could really use your help," she said to the clerk at the front desk, a woman with finely shaped brows and fading lipstick. "I have an older woman here who's lost. She doesn't seem to speak English and I don't know where to put her."

"Okay. Where is she?"

Marina turned and nodded at the woman, whose feet barely reached the ground. "She's sitting right there."

The clerk looked in the direction Marina gestured to and frowned. "Where?"

"Right there," she pointed, not understanding the other woman's confusion since there was no one else there. "The woman right there."

"What woman?" the clerk said suddenly cautious, licking the rest of her faded lipstick from her mouth.

Marina turned and saw the older woman flash a strange smile. "You don't see her?"

"Do you need somewhere to stay?"

"No, I'm fine."

"Have you been drinking?"

"No."

"Taking anything?"

"I'm perfectly lucid." *At least I think so.* Her mother's suggestion was playing with her thoughts. It couldn't be. How could she have picked up a witch? They didn't exist. Not like this. They weren't invisible. Then why couldn't anyone else see or hear her?

She turned to the woman. "Why are you doing this to me? At least say something."

Her smile remained.

"What have I done wrong to deserve this?"

The clerk cleared her throat. "Why don't you just take a seat? I'll get someone to help you."

Marina spun around and glared at her. "I'm not crazy."

"Of course you're not," the clerk said in an indulgent tone.

Marina was about to take umbrage with her tone when a man came from around the corner. He looked as if he'd had a worse night than she'd had. He hadn't shaved in a while and his tie had the crooked look of a man who just didn't care. If Marina had been in the mood she would have noticed that he was good looking, in a rugged way, but she just didn't care. She wanted to get rid of the old woman and go back to sleep. Or wake up from this nightmare, whichever was faster.

"Idris what's the name of the local shelter?" the clerk asked.

"It's going to be pretty full," he said. "What's that other lady here for?"

The clerk stared at him stunned.

Marina jumped with joy, wanting to grab his sleeve but refraining. She wasn't imagining things. "You see her too?"

He sent her an odd look. "Of course I see her. She's sitting right there. How could I miss her?"

The clerk shook her head. "Idris you've had a long night."

"I know."

"There's no one there."

"Maybe you need a rest. It's two to one."

"There's one way to decide this." The clerk took out her phone and took a picture. Then she grinned with triumph. "I'm right." She turned the image to them. They saw the wall and an empty chair.

Marina turned to the woman then the image on the tiny screen. "I don't believe this."

"There's something wrong with your camera," Idris said.

The clerk took the phone and tucked it away. "It's Christmas Eve and it's a crazy night, weird things happen. I think you two should just go home. "

The older woman leaped to her feet. "Yes, it's time," she said in perfect English. Then she grabbed Marina's hand and Idris's.

"What are you doing?" Idris said.

"You speak English?" Marina said at the same time.

They both looked at the woman then each other with a mixture of fear and awe then their world went black.

Chapter Five

When Idris Helmond came to, he didn't know how to feel. One moment he was thinking about closing a case on the brutal beating of a gas station attendant and finding the right gift to make his girlfriend, Deena, happy. She was pissed about something, but that wasn't new. She was always pissed about something and she wouldn't tell him why, she'd only let him know he was the cause. Then he'd seen the pretty young woman trying to find shelter for an older woman who looked strangely cunning.

He didn't know where he was or what to think. He looked around him and saw the neat road and manicured lawns of a neighborhood. The place felt familiar. He looked around and spotted a house— It was his sister's house. Beautifully decorated for the holidays. But he knew it wasn't like that now. That house was no longer hers. The scene was from three years ago. He shook his head in rising dread and took a hasty step back. "No, no. What are we doing here?"

"You have to be here," the older woman said.

"No, I don't. I know what happens. I don't need to be here. Let's go."

"Idris."

He threw up his hand, his voice in a near panic. "I said I don't want to be here."

"What is this place?" Marina asked.

"It doesn't matter, let's go." But the woman wouldn't release her hold and she had the strength to keep him there. "Get us out of here whoever—or whatever you are," he said in his best 'or you'll regret this' tone.

But the older woman didn't release him.

He turned and saw a woman march up to the front door as if on a mission. She flipped through the many keys on her keychain before she got the right one. She placed the key in the lock then turned the handle with an angry twist. "No. Don't go in there. Please." He turned to the older woman, feeling as if he could no longer breathe. "Make her stop."

"I can't."

"Then why did you bring me here?"

"Haven't you been playing this scene over in your mind for three years? Haven't you already remembered and replayed every detail? Isn't this the reason you won't see your nephews? Why you make excuses not to visit your parents every holiday season? You're here because this is where you're stuck. This is where you stopped your life too. Your sister got twenty-five to life, but you're living a life sentence by staying in a job you hate because it makes your parents proud. Staying in a relationship that is soulless. You chose this. When are you going to get past this moment? A moment that will never change?"

"She shouldn't have had keys to his place. Why did it have to happen? She was my baby sister and I couldn't stop her. "

"No. She was a woman who'd made a choice."

"I gave her the gun to protect herself."

"She used it for something else. Your sister couldn't except that her ex had remarried, that he'd created a new life for himself. Just like you, she couldn't move on. She was convicted because she hadn't snapped. She decided to pick up the kids early. She decided to catch her ex with his new love and she decided to shoot them both dead."

They heard a scream and then three pops.

"You couldn't have stopped it," the older woman said.

Idris fell to his knees, losing all strength, as if he'd been shot too. The awful part was the guilt. Her husband had been his best friend. He'd felt the loss from the divorce too. His sister had been married to Nathanial for ten years and he'd been a good father to their two sons. He'd been someone Idris had admired. He'd expected Nathanial to be his best man one day. He'd seen them as the perfect couple until the cracks began to show.

He remembered his brother-in-law complaining about his sister's drinking and shopping sprees. He remembered Nathanial getting full custody of the children. Idris understood the judge's ruling, his sister had become unstable, but he still had divided loyalties, even though it was best for the boys. His parents had remained blind wanting to see their precious little girl as the victim and Nathanial as the villain. But he knew it wasn't as black and white as that. Just like his nephews, his world had been shattered that day. He'd buried someone who'd been like a brother and lost his sister too. She was still bitter, even in prison. She still blamed the system for not understanding her rage. His parents blamed him for not seeing the signs sooner. For somehow not stopping it.

"The season had nothing to do with her choice," the older woman said.

"Really?" he said with a sneer. "You know the rates of murders go up around the holidays?"

"Was it the holidays that put the liquor down her throat or the gun in her hand?"

"She snapped because she felt so alone," Idris said trying to rationalize something he knew he couldn't. "She felt disconnected. It's a season that feeds discontentment. Domestic violence cases practically sky rocket. A time of good cheer my ass. People find even more reasons to hate each other."

"Remember when you and Nathanial took your nephews sledding? Remember the time when you both laughed at the instructions for putting together a racecar track? You had joy. That joy was real. It's okay to love your sister and hate what she did. Your friend wouldn't want you to throw away all the good times just for this moment. You have to get past this."

"I don't know how," he said his voice raw. He glanced at the younger woman, who stood motionless beside the other woman, wondering why he'd chosen to share this nightmare with her.

"You can do it by looking at this place one last time. And saying goodbye."

"My parents blame me and his parents won't talk to me."

"You shut Nathanial's parents out of your life as much as you have your nephews. And they miss you. Don't let the memory of their father die. You don't have to replace him. But make his life mean more than his death. Don't let your sister's bitterness rob you too."

A purple fog quickly swept over the scene and soon they stood in front of Nathanial's grave. A light dusting of snow fell from the blanket of white clouds, but Idris didn't feel cold. He didn't feel anything. He brushed the snow from the headstone then gathered some and let it melt between his fingers. He remembered introducing Nathanial to his sister and the instant attraction between them. He remembered his sister telling him about their first date. He remembered their wedding day and visiting the hospital when Nathanial held their first son and the pride and joy on his face.

Tears filled and stung his eyes as he recalled the fights, the tense phone calls, the divorce proceeding and then his sister's conviction. Both he and Nathanial had been detectives, determined to help and serve others, but hadn't been able to fix their own lives. Idris tasted the tears though he didn't feel them streaming down his face. "I'm so sorry," he said, then he felt the cold against his skin, the wetness on his cheeks. He felt his loss, his rage and his despair.

"He's forgiven you," the old woman said. "He wants you to know that. Now you have to forgive yourself."

Idris wiped his tears then fell to his knees feeling like a broken man. "I can't."

"Because you're afraid. You're afraid that if it couldn't go right for him, it won't for you. So you won't even try. But you're wrong. You can have the life you want. You know Nathanial knew there were signs early on that the relationship wouldn't work. He told you some of them but he chose to ignore them. I'm not saying he's responsible, but there are gray areas that none of you could see. Some you didn't want to see."

Idris nodded. "I know."

"Now say the name of his favorite holiday song."

"No."

"Say it, then say goodbye."

He shook his head. "It's stupid."

"Say it anyway."

He sighed. "*I Want a Hippopotamus for Christmas.*"

Marina giggled then covered her mouth embarrassed, but Idris heard it anyway and couldn't help a smile. He'd forgotten she was there and he felt awkward that she'd seen him at such a fragile time. He was used to keeping his emotions bottled up, but when he looked at her, he didn't feel that she was judging him and that made his awkwardness disappear. Made him glad he wasn't alone. "The idiot," he said with fondness. "He loved that song and knew all the words. He'd hum it just to annoy me."

"Sounds like a fun guy."

"He was. He loved the holidays. Everything about it."

Marina kneeled beside him and tentatively took his hand, half expecting him to pull away. "I'm sorry."

He squeezed her hand and released a deep shuddering breathe, as if he'd been holding it a long time. "Thanks."

"Do you really hate your job?" she asked.

"Yes, every single day I feel like I'm dying."

"Then why don't you change it?"

He sent her a look of surprise. "You think it's that easy?"

"No, but it's better than feeling like this."

"Tell her what you want," the old woman said.

He stood and dusted snow from his trousers although he didn't need to. Although the ground was powered with snow, his trousers remained dry. "No."

"Are you afraid to?"

"Yes."

"Tell her later then." The old woman turned to Marina. "Now it's your turn."

"I guess I don't have a choice," she said with a grimace before their world went black.

Chapter Six

After seeing Idris's past, Marina prepared herself for a painful holiday memory. So when she saw the sight of her old bakery kitchen she couldn't help her surprise. She stared at the sight of the woman she'd been four years ago. The kitchen was small, all her new equipment that Eli would encourage her to purchase hadn't filled the room yet. She saw herself stirring something in a bowl and humming. She then scooped the contents into a tube and decorated cookies with a flair of fun. Her efforts weren't perfect, but she didn't seem to mind. Marina gaped at her younger self with wonder. She didn't remember even being that happy.

"What are we doing here?" Marina asked. "I already know I'm going to fail. I already know this isn't what I'm meant to do."

The old woman held up one finger. "Just wait."

Marina folded her arms, feeling impatient. She didn't want to wait. She wanted to leave. She wanted to go back to sleep and forget this day ever happened. She was about to comment to the fact when Eli walked into the room. Eli the man she'd thought she'd loved and who she'd thought loved her and her dreams. The man who'd told her he'd support her through thick and thin. The one who'd later embezzle her funds and leave her heart broken.

"What are you doing?"

"Working on a new icing."

He frowned "You're still trying that?"

"I want to make it work."

"You're wasting your time. Why don't you just focus on what will make money?"

For the first time Marina noticed how he hadn't greeted her and how much he didn't look pleased. Why hadn't she seen that before? He was only about making money. He didn't care what she did. He didn't care about her passion. She loved baking, she'd forgotten about that. She'd let him douse her hopes and leave an empty shell.

But the younger version of herself didn't know this. She gave him a taste of the icing.

He made a face and shook his head. "It's still not up to standard. You know you're no good at this. I told you to stick with simple things. Why won't you listen?"

"I wanted to give customers a new experience."

"This isn't a culinary institute. You're not making art. Just bake cookies and cakes and you'll be in the black instead of the red. Now let's go."

Marina saw the light in her eyes dim.

"Who is this jerk?" Idris said.

"The man I thought I'd marry," Marina said.

"Oh, sorry."

"Me too."

She saw her younger self watch Eli leave the kitchen and then she took all her experiments and dumped them into the trash.

"That was the moment you let him steal your dream," the old woman said.

Marina let her hands fall to her sides. "My dream failed. I failed. The business flopped. Even if he hadn't taken the money he was right, I was no good."

"But you were getting better. You stopped trying. You listened to him when you should have ignored him. He didn't support you. He lied to you and you believed his lies. What if you'd kept experimenting and one of them worked? You started to make your business just about money and not about joy. That was when you gave up on your dream. Your dream never gave up on you." The old woman pointed to the trash bin. "This is the moment you failed."

Marina twisted her lips and shrugged. "It's too late now."

The old woman took Marina's hand and patted it. "You're too young to start speaking like an old woman. Even if you were my age it wouldn't be too late to live with joy. To try. To dream." The old woman looked at Idris. "Are you ready to tell her what you've always wanted to do?"

"No."

She sighed.

"Why won't you tell me?" Marina asked. "We'll never see each other again. Are you afraid because you'll fail like I did?"

He shoved his hands in his pockets and looked away.

Marina looked at the old woman. "I don't understand any of this." She glanced around the kitchen that was no longer hers. A past that still caused her pain. "Why are you showing us things we can't change?"

"Because that's the point. You can't change the past, but the future is yours. You don't have to be stuck here. The holidays are full of presents. Not just the gifts given to each other, but the moments you inhabit every day. They matter. The choices you make matter. Make your presents matter, then the future will belong to you. You just have to believe it."

Marina bit her lip then squinted at her. "What are you?"

"Does it matter?"

"Why couldn't I understand you before?"

"Because you weren't ready to."

"Why us?"

The old woman kissed her teeth with annoyance. "You ask such silly questions. Why not you? If I am a spirit or a ghost or your imagination does it matter? Those questions aren't important. The important question is: What will you do next?"

"Will we remember any of this?"

She just smiled.

Idris rested his hands on his hips. "What should we do next?"

Her smile just widened.

"I think that's all she'll tell us," Marina said. "This is what she did to me when we first met."

"I guess it's a sign that our journey is coming to an end."

"Yes." Marina glanced at his tie and had a strange urge to straighten it, but resisted. She lifted her gaze to his face. He had a nice face and she wished she could know him better. After Eli's betrayal, she hadn't wanted to know another man. "Whatever happens, good luck to you. I hope that you'll see your nephews this year."

"And you should keep baking, if it makes you happy."

"It does." She tilted her head to the side. "And what did you always want to do?"

This time he only smiled but for the first time she saw a twinkle in his eye.

"Fine, don't tell me. Good luck with that too."

"Thanks."

The old woman took both their hands and they shared a look—this time with hope and anticipation—then the world went black.

Chapter Seven

The phone call shattered a beautiful dream at 3a.m. on Christmas Eve. Marina groggily reached for the phone hoping that it would stop ringing by the time she picked up. It didn't.

"Hello?"

"I'm sorry to wake you," her mother said. "But I need you to pick up Uncle Sola."

"Who?"

"Uncle Sola. He'll be arriving at BWI and—"

"Mom I can't keep doing this."

"I know and I feel bad but I know you're off all week."

"Off?" Was she trying to be funny? She wasn't off. She didn't have a job.

"Yes, you and the boys are going to Delaware. Just this quick favor and I won't do it again." She gave the flight number and description then hung up.

Delaware? Boys? Her words vaguely made sense but then they didn't make sense at all. Her mind felt as though it was between a dream and a wake state.

"What was that about?" a deep voice said beside her.

Marina froze. She knew that voice, but yet she didn't know it. And what was he doing in her bed? She slowly turned to him. Idris. Not the sad, tired Idris from the police station. He looked sleepy, but happy.

She pushed her sheets away. "I have to go pick someone up from the airport."

He frowned and put the sheets back. "No, you're not."

"My mother."

"Give me the phone."

"But—"

He reached across her, grabbed the phone and dialed. "Hi Mom. Sorry she can't make it. Tell him to take a taxi and I'll pay for the tab. Yes, I know. I don't care. Then get Wale to do it. Yes. Okay, bye." He disconnected and handed her the phone.

Marina gripped the phone in two hands. "What did she say?"

"Relax. You don't have to go."

He'd called her mother 'Mom'. Yes, because he was her husband. That felt right. Yes, they were married. Why had she ever imagined him sad? And she'd never been in a police station. Where had that thought come from? The dream state faded and everything became clear. They'd been married a year. He used to be a detective and now he was a real estate developer, raising his two nephews. She did catering: Sweet desserts. She wasn't making lots of money but she was happy and he always let her practice her experiments on him and the boys loved to be in the kitchen with her. She suddenly remembered snow ball fights and searching for a tree. But most of all she remembered meeting him one Christmas day.

He'd taken his nephews to a birthday party a friend had invited her to cater and their eyes met over a row of cupcakes and for her it felt like she'd known him from somewhere. Like they'd known each other forever. She still felt that way.

Marina settled back under the warm sheets. There was a question that niggled her mind. She didn't know why, but for some reason she wanted to know the answer. She had to. "What have you always wanted to do?"

Idris was slow to answer and at first she thought he may have fallen back asleep.

He hadn't. He felt as if someone had asked him that question before and he'd had a hard time answering. But now he wanted to. He looked around the cozy bedroom knowing his nephews were safe and asleep in their beds, the presents were under the tree ready to be opened. He could already taste the maple syrup covered waffles Marina would make for breakfast. He looked at his wife, his friend, unsure he could put into words all they'd asked for. He'd wanted to follow his heart and take care of his nephews, build a business that would support his family and find a woman he wasn't afraid to love. One he could trust. A woman who'd love him just as he was.

Idris drew her close, amazed that he'd gotten all that he'd ever dreamed. "This," he said then tenderly placed his lips against hers.

And the next morning on top of the Christmas tree, Marina saw an angel that wasn't the same one she'd put there several weeks ago. It didn't have wings, instead it wore a brightly colored headwrap, matching dress and a big smile.

The Gift Box

"So what do you think?"

Tamara Cole stared at the box and didn't exactly know what to think of the present her husband, Ross, had given her. She'd torn through the brightly colored green and gold wrapping paper that Christmas Eve and lifted the lid, giddy with expectation. The size of the box had been too large to be jewelry, certainly too small to be a TV, but still large enough to get her imagination spinning. Even before she'd lifted the box, she'd come up with a series of guesses.

The soccer ball sized square box could have been the stack of new plush towels she'd wanted, a silk robe and pajama set she'd been eyeing, perhaps something for the baby they planned to welcome in four months. Maybe it was a set of lavender bath lotions, she really wanted to pamper herself with during the times when she felt a little dumpy. Although she was excited about becoming a mother, she was also a little nervous too. There was so much she didn't know.

This Christmas would be their last as a couple and Ross had helped her make it special. They'd gotten a tall, fresh evergreen tree, which stood boldly near the window. A lovely sight every time they arrived home. She'd bought extra garlands for the hallway, a wreath so large it covered half of the front door and a welcome mat showing a picture of a holly bush that lit up when people stepped on it.

She looked forward to the Christmas dinner tomorrow evening, when her parents, and her sister and her family, would arrive, but this Christmas Eve belonged to them. They sat together on the carpet in front of the tree, in the hushed silence of the evening, the ticking clock the only other sound in the room. It was supposed to be a night she'd remember forever, a gift that would bring tears of joy to her face.

Instead...instead...he'd given her this? Tamara stared inside the box speechless.

"Honey, what do you think?" he asked again.

Honey? He dared to call her that? "I don't know what to think," she said, stumbling over the words, not sure if she should laugh or cry. Anger mingled with annoyance and disbelief.

"I know," he said with a proud grin. "Isn't it amazing? I didn't think I'd get one. You can image how hard it was, but I was determined."

Tamara set the box on the ground, stunned her husband could mock her with such a goofy expression on his handsome brown face. Why was he smiling? "I don't think it's funny."

His smile wavered. "It wasn't meant to be funny."

"Then what's an empty box supposed to be?"

His smile disappeared. "Empty?"

She nodded. "Yes, empty."

"How could it be empty?" He reached for the box and looked inside then stared at her, his brown eyes stunned. "It's right there. Don't you see it?"

Tamara looked inside again. Was he playing some sort of cruel joke? She didn't see anything. Just the white interior of a square cube. "No."

He frowned. "Maybe we should get your eyes checked."

"Maybe we should get your head checked," she shot back. She lifted the box. "This is completely empty," she said and began to turn it upside down to prove her point.

He reached out and stopped her. "Don't do that!" He took the box from her and gently set it down beside him. "You'll damage it. You have to be very careful. It wasn't easy to get you know."

She surged to her feet. "I'm not playing this silly game anymore."

He stared up at her. "It's not a game."

She pointed at the box. "There's nothing in there." She took a deep breath then rested her hands on her hips. "Ross, don't do this. You know how important this evening is to me. She smoothed down her blue and silver blouse, which she'd worn especially for the evening, and rested her hands at her sides. She would be calm. "Now where's my real present?"

Ross looked at her for a long moment, resting his arm on his extended leg. "This gift is what I got you." He gestured to the box. "It's all that I got you. I thought you'd…" He furrowed his brows. "You really don't see it?"

She didn't understand why he wouldn't back down, but she didn't care. "No, and when my family doesn't see it too, you'd better make sure my *real* present is spectacular."

***

As she set the table for dinner the following evening, a part of Tamara regretted making the suggestion. She didn't want to expose her husband's silly prank to her family. She'd hoped that after she'd challenged him, he would have said, "No, there's no need to do that," and then give her her real gift. But instead, he'd nodded grimly and said, "Fine," before clearing the wrapping paper away.

Ross showed everyone the box after dessert. Tamara had been left to watch a holiday cartoon with her niece and nephew, aged three and five, when Ross had taken her parents, sister Carrie and her husband into another room and showed them the gift. He'd told her that the gift wasn't appropriate for children their age. She heard their collective gasp from the other room. Her mother then spoke in a tone filled with awe, although Tamara couldn't make out the words, her father's low grumble sounded equally amazed.

When they all returned to the family room, Ross sent her a look saying, "See? I told you," before her mother told her how lucky she was. Tamara couldn't believe it. They'd all seen it? How could that be? Why was she the only one who couldn't see it? Were they all just pretending?

These questions swirled in her mind as she cleared up the kitchen. Then her sister Carrie came in and offered to help.

Her older sister Carrie had done everything right. Carrie, with her six figure salary, vacation house, master's degree and svelte physique—smooth mocha skin and dark twists which fell to her shoulders. Carrie, with her two great kids and husband. Carrie, who succeeded even when she wasn't trying. Tamara watched her sister enter her tiny kitchen wearing jeans and a satin red top, looking like a woman who hired someone else to handle her stress. Even with two kids and a high powered job she looked calm and confident.

Tamara both admired and envied her. As much as she tried to follow the same path as her sister, she always fell short. She'd married later than her sister—early thirties instead of late twenties. She'd started a family later than planned—three years instead of two, she hadn't graduated from university with honors. She hadn't graduated at all, dropping out in her third year. She worked as a bookkeeper for her husband's furniture restoration business. Not a glamorous role nor as lucrative as being the vice president of a bank.

She didn't have a housekeeper to keep her place spotless, her dinner parties weren't talked about months later and now…now her sister (and her parents) saw a gift Ross had given her, a gift that she still couldn't see. And when she glanced down at the red blouse she'd chosen for the evening—why did it have to be red?—she felt as round and ridiculous as a Christmas ornament.

"What was the first thing you did when you saw it?" Carrie asked Tamara as she helped her load dishes stained yellow and red from curried chicken and jollof rice into the dishwasher.

Tamara scratched the back of her ear. "I was so…happy I just hugged him."

Carrie looked at her for a long moment then rested her hip against the counter and folded her arms. "You don't see it, do you?"

Tamara's chest tightened. She felt caught, exposed. Her throat tightened. She struggled to swallow. She couldn't let her sister know the truth. Anybody else, her parents, her friends, people in other countries, but not her. "Yes, I do."

Carrie sent her a look that made it clear she knew Tamara was lying, but she shrugged her shoulder before continuing loading the dishes. "I wish my husband got me a gift like that. What do you plan to do?"

"I don't know." She hesitated. "What would you do?"

A self-satisfied smile touched Carrie's lips. "Doesn't matter, it's not my gift."

Tamara rubbed her hands knowing that look, that smile, her innocent question had exposed the truth, but she didn't care. She'd had to take a risk. She truly wanted to know what was in the box and what her sister would do with it. But her sister wouldn't help her. She'd keep the knowledge a secret. Her sister, who always knew everything. Tamara made a face at her sister when Carrie looked down to turn on the dishwasher. Did she have to sound so smug? Couldn't she give her a hint?

The dishwasher hummed to life.

"But there is one thing you should do," Carrie said, looking at her.

"What?" Tamara asked, hoping her expression did not betray her.

Her gaze turned serious, her words heartfelt. "Cherish him. A man like Ross doesn't come along every day."

***

Did the gift have something to do with Ross? Was that what she was missing? Tamara sat up in bed, drumming her fingers on her rounded belly, ruminating over her sister's words instead of looking at the wood crafter's magazine on her lap. She stole a glance at Ross while he sat beside her with his eyes closed while he listened to an audiobook. She didn't know how he could do that. She'd tried it once and had fallen asleep, but it was his favorite nightly ritual.

She studied his profile and sighed. Why had her sister mentioned her husband instead of the gift? Were they one in the same? She clasped her hands together as a thought came to her. She tapped him on the shoulder.

He took off his headset and looked at her questioning.

"Okay, I get it now," she said. "It's symbolic. It's a box of your love or your affection. It's something that's there but I haven't been paying attention to because I've been preparing for the baby so I haven't seen it, right? Is that what you're telling me?"

He set his headset aside and sighed. "It's not invisible, honey. It's not something I made up. It's real and tangible."

Her buoyant mood faded, she'd hoped she'd solved the mystery. Instead she'd failed. She stared down at an ad in the magazine for wood polish, hating the look of disappointment in his gaze. She hated disappointing him. She didn't even know what she'd done wrong. Why couldn't she see his gift?

"Maybe you can't see it because of the baby," he said. "Maybe that's interfering with it." He patted her hand. "Don't worry about it and go to sleep." He put his headset back on.

She didn't want to admit defeat. She didn't want to admit that the problem wasn't his gift, but her. It made her question too much. Was this why her life hadn't followed the timeline she'd planned? Was this why they were still living in a little green apple colored colonial instead of the grand Georgian she'd thought she'd be living in by now? Would she be a good mother? Did he think she was a good wife. A good worker? Did he know how hard she tried to make it all work?

Tangible. He'd said it was real and tangible. She'd never tried to touch it before.

Tamara left the bedroom and returned to the gift box she'd left under the tree. The box felt so light, how could anything possibly be inside it? She lifted the lid, reached her hand inside and felt nothing.

Then something, soft like a feather or the wings of a butterfly, brushed against her fingers. Or was that just a breeze? She tried again and felt it again. She yanked her hand out. There *was* something inside, but why couldn't she see it? *What* was it?

She pretended to sleep that night, but cried instead. She cried quietly so that Ross wouldn't notice. She let the tears fall and bit her lip hard so she wouldn't make a sound. It was supposed to be a happy day—a happy season—but her heart felt shattered.

***

"I didn't mean to make you cry," Ross said the next morning at breakfast as he set a plate of seasoned eggs, spinach and baked plantain in front of her.

"I don't know what you mean," Tamara said, lifting her fork.

"Don't lie to me."

She set her fork down ashamed. She'd tried to hide her red puffy eyes with makeup. Clearly her attempt at camouflage had failed.

"One lie is enough," he said before she could apologize.

She blinked shocked. "What lie? When?"

"When you told me you believed in them."

Tamara felt her blood grow cold as she met his steady, penetrating gaze. Suddenly she knew what she should have seen: A sula. A fairy that only appears to believers. They never show themselves to those who pretend. They reveal a person's true heart. And she'd been exposed as a fraud. She'd heard the stories about them as a child, learned that their presence had first been noticed centuries ago in a village located off the tip of West Africa. No one was quite sure which country—it shifted depending on the storyteller. Most Westerners disregarded them because they were quiet, shy and didn't travel in groups as other known fairies tended to.

She opened her mouth desperately wanting to say, "I saw it a little bit," but closed her mouth knowing that would be a lie. And she didn't want to lie to him again.

A shot of anger coursed through her. How could this be happening? Why had he tested her? Why had he used such a big box for something so small? How could she have guessed? But just as quickly her anger disappeared, the fact that she couldn't see it wasn't his fault. He'd tried to surprise her. Just as he had when he'd proposed to her on her birthday, presenting her with a big box with a tiny engagement ring inside, tied to a red rose.

Her sister was right—it was an amazing gift. Sulas only appeared around the holidays to special people. But it hadn't revealed itself to her. What did this mean? How would Ross look at her now? Would he trust her again?

She hadn't exactly lied when he'd first asked her whether she believed in them. She was so in love, everything seemed rosy and possible then. She'd loved him and didn't think that it mattered. But would he trust her again after this?

"I used to believe once," she said, desperate to fill the silence. "When I was a child then...I let it go."

His gaze fell to his plate but not fast enough to hide the glimmer of sadness hidden there. "They only stay three days and then disappear. I had hoped you'd get a wish, but I guess..."

"I will. I'll get a wish. Please give me a chance."

He reached over and patted her hand in the same reassuring way he had last night, but instead of feeling comfort, it stung. "Never mind. I'll get you something else tomorrow."

***

She didn't want another gift. She wanted this one. This mattered more than anything he could buy at a store.

Later that day, Tamara knelt in front of the box. "Please show yourself to me, I *do* believe. I have to believe." After a moment she added, "If not for me then for Ross. He means so much to me and it would make him so happy."

But no matter how much she begged nothing appeared.

She felt a light touch on her shoulder. "Darling, come to bed, you've been here nearly all day."

She hadn't noticed. It didn't matter. Nothing else mattered. "I'll be there in a minute."

"Tamara."

"If Carrie can see it, I must see it too."

"This is not a competition."

Yes it is, she wanted to say, but he wouldn't understand. She couldn't have her sister achieve something else she couldn't. She had to prove that she was a good wife; didn't he know how much his disappointment hurt her?

She shrugged his hand away. "Please, just leave me alone." *I have to do this!* She only had one day left.

She felt a feather-light kiss on her forehead then heard his footsteps fade away upstairs.

She wanted to believe again. She wanted to feel the magic again and trust in it. She closed her eyes and willed her heart to see what was there, but when she opened her eyes the box was still empty.

She clasped her hands together in a plea and squeezed her eyes shut as night swallowed up day until only the glow of the tree dotted the room with tiny lights. "I need just one look. One glance. I wish I could see you if only for a moment."

She heard nothing move, she felt nothing happen. She opened her eyes, her heart sinking at the sight of the still empty box.

"I'm not in there anymore you know," a tiny voice said.

Tamara glanced up and saw a tiny brown fairy sitting crossed-legged on a branch, her wings a shimmering green gold, her skin the color of chestnut, her dark hair coiled into an elaborate braid.

Tamara stared wide-eyed, her heart racing. "You're real."

"Of course I'm real."

"And beautiful."

"Naturally, and I don't have much time either."

"Yes, I know. I get to make my wish," Tamara said with eagerness. What should she wish for first? Something for her baby or for humankind or…?

The sula swung her foot. "You already made your wish."

Tamara frowned. "No, I didn't."

"You wished with all your heart that you would be able to see me." She opened her arms wide. "And now you can."

"But—"

She wagged her finger, a little gold bracelet swaying on her arm. "Those are the rules. I made your wish come true." She folded her arms and shrugged her tiny shoulders. "It's not my fault you wasted your wish on something so simple."

Tamara waited for a feeling of anger to hit her—yes she'd wasted time, so much time—but instead she didn't feel anything, but relief. The sula was right, it was her fault that she'd lost the ability to see what was there. It was her fault she'd stopped believing.

But that evening, she'd been given new eyes. Eyes to see all the gifts that surrounded her in brilliant glory: Her husband. The new life that would soon join them. Her family. Instead of a house that was too small, she saw a beautiful home—with its dark shutters and snow dusted driveway—that was just right for them.

Soon her gaze sharpened to extend beyond her and she now saw that'd she'd been running a race of her own making, that life wasn't a competition; that being amazed by her sister's accomplishments didn't make hers—a thriving business and growing customer base—any less wonderful. And beyond herself and her town she heard it speak— Peace. Peace in its silence—free from the sound of bomb blasts, gun shots, screams, cries, roaring tanks, police and ambulance sirens—filled her being. Peace amid life's horrors restored her.

Her eyes filled with tears of joy mingled with shame. She'd been blind to so many things. She'd been blind to true happiness. "Thank you. Thank you for everything."

The sula smiled then stood and bowed before disappearing. Lights suddenly flooded the room.

Tamara looked around as if waking from a dream.

"Are you talking to yourself again?" Ross asked behind her.

She jumped to her feet and hugged him. "I saw her! I saw her and she's wonderful."

He held her close."Really?"

"She had a tiny little voice, gold bracelets on both wrists, white slippered shoes and soft fairy wings."

Ross didn't reply, but she felt the tension in him—between them—relax. "I'm glad you saw her."

She drew back and looked at him. "Now I see so many things." She cupped his face. "I see how lucky I am to have you. To have this," she said motioning to the room and everything that it meant. "And so much more. Your gift is something I will never forget."

And four months later when her baby girl was born, Tamara saw a special sparkle in her daughter's brown gaze and knew she'd never be blind to life's magic again.

About the Author

Dara Girard, the award-winning, bestselling author of more than thirty novels, continues to gain new readers with novels such as *Just One Look*, *Dangerous Curves* and *The Amber Stone*. Dara loves to travel and hear from readers.

You can write her at:
contactdara@daragirard.com
or
P.O. Box 10345
Silver Spring, MD 20914

If you'd like to receive a reply, please send a self-addressed stamped envelope. Visit daragirard.com to join her newsletter and be the first to find out about current and upcoming releases.

Other Books by Dara

If you enjoyed the short stories in this collection you may also enjoy Dara's novels.

If you liked *The Perfect Christmas* then try…
The Sapphire Pendant
The Amber Stone

If you liked *The Special Guest* then try…
The Daughters of Winston Barnett

If you liked *A Cup of Cheer* then try…
Table for Two
Gaining Interest

If you liked *New Year's Surprise* then try…
Playing for Keeps
After Hours
A Private Affair
Just One Look